CHAPTER 1	
CHAPTER 2	**16**
CHAPTER 3	**28**
CHAPTER 4	**40**
CHAPTER 5	**53**
CHAPTER 6	**65**
CHAPTER 7	**77**
CHAPTER 8	**91**
CHAPTER 9	**105**
CHAPTER 10	**118**
CHAPTER 11	**130**
CHAPTER 12	**143**
CHAPTER 13	**156**
CHAPTER 14	**168**

CHAPTER 15	181
CHAPTER 16	194
CHAPTER 17	207
CHAPTER 18	219
CHAPTER 19	232
CHAPTER 20	244
CHAPTER 21	256
CHAPTER 22	268
EPILOGUE	281
OTHER BOOKS BY LEENA CLOVER	287
ACKNOWLEDGEMENTS	288
JOIN MY NEWSLETTER	289

Chapter 1

Jenny King dipped a warm donut in strawberry glaze and swirled it around. She placed it on a wire rack and smiled to herself, thinking about her new home.

"Don't forget the sprinkles," Heather Morse, Jenny's friend, reminded her as she entered the kitchen.

At forty four, Jenny had completely reinvented herself. Dumped by her husband of twenty years, she had grabbed her aunt's invitation to come visit her like a lifeline. She had arrived in the small seaside town of Pelican Cove to lick her wounds. After letting her wallow for a few days, her aunt had coaxed her into helping out at the local café, just to keep busy. The rest, as they said, was history.

The Boardwalk Café had always been a landmark in Pelican Cove. Jenny's presence added a Midas touch and kicked it up a few notches. Thanks to the Internet and social media, her fame had spread quickly. People were coming from far and wide to sample her food. Jenny didn't disappoint them, churning out tasty recipes that used the abundant local seafood and fresh produce.

The strawberry glazed donuts were her latest creation and people couldn't stop ordering them.

"You're early," Jenny said lightly.

"Grandma's feeling a bit poorly," Heather explained. "She's staying home with Tootsie."

Tootsie was Heather's black poodle, adorable but totally spoilt.

"What's wrong with Betty Sue?" Jenny's brows furrowed in concern.

Betty Sue Morse, Heather's grandmother, was the fourth generation descendant of James Morse, the first owner and inhabitant of the island. It had been called Morse Isle then.

James Morse of New England travelled south with his wife Caroline and his three children in 1837. He bought the island for $125 and named it Morse Isle. He built a house for his family on a large tract of land. Fishing provided him with a livelihood, so did floating wrecks. He sent for a friend or two from up north. They came and settled on the island with their families. They in turn invited their friends. Morse Isle soon became a thriving community.

Being a barrier island, it took a battering in the great storm of 1962. Half the island was submerged forever. Most of that land had belonged to the Morse family. A new town emerged in the aftermath of the storm and it was named Pelican Cove.

Betty Sue was a force to reckon with in Pelican Cove. Well into her eighties, she ran the Bayview Inn and the whole town with a vigor that would shame someone half her age.

"It's the weather," Heather shrugged. "She's coming down with a cold, I guess."

October in the coastal Virginia town was milder than in the north. But the temperatures had dropped suddenly. Islanders could be seen wearing an extra layer. Jenny herself didn't feel the cold in the warm kitchen.

"I'm making pumpkin soup today. I'll save some for Betty Sue."

"You'll have to bring it to her yourself," Heather told her. "I have a date."

Jenny refused to comment.

Heather was a recent convert to online dating. She had finally confided in her grandmother about it. It hadn't gone down well.

"Who are you seeing this time?" Jenny piped up.

"It's a first date," Heather admitted.

"How many first dates have you been on in the last few weeks?" Jenny asked.

Petunia Clark, the owner of the Boardwalk Café, breezed in and started a fresh pot of coffee.

"They are here," she told the girls.

A group of women met for coffee around ten each morning at the Boardwalk Café. They called themselves the Magnolias. Petunia Clark, Betty Sue Morse and Jenny's aunt Star were the older generation. Jenny, Heather and their friend Molly completed the group. Jenny treasured their friendship and would do anything for this group of women.

Jenny carried a tray of donuts out to the deck overlooking the Atlantic Ocean.

"Have you moved all your stuff in?" Molly Henderson asked, biting into a warm strawberry glazed donut.

"Nick's bringing some of my things over from the city," Jenny told the ladies.

Jenny's son Nick was a college freshman. Luckily, he had been over eighteen when Jenny separated from her husband. He visited Jenny regularly and spent a lot of time in Pelican Cove.

"Your husband agreed to it?" Molly asked.

"What's he going to do with my clothes?" Jenny asked. "Nick's also getting some mementos, old photos and some of his trophies from school. They will look fine on the mantel at Seaview."

Seaview was an imposing three storey house facing the ocean. It was right next to her aunt Star's cottage. Jenny had fallen in love with the old house and bought it with her divorce settlement. Seaview had been lying abandoned for over twenty five years. Everyone had been surprised when they learned Jenny was planning to make it her home.

"I wish you weren't moving out," Star muttered.

She had grown used to Jenny in the past few months.

"I'm not moving out alone," Jenny reminded her. "We are both moving out."

Jenny had invited Star to come live with her at Seaview. The house was big enough. Star was a local artist who painted landscapes and seascapes of the surrounding region. Her work was popular among the tourists who thronged to the island every year. She had her own art gallery in town and it did brisk business. Jenny had turned part of the third floor into a studio for Star. With tall glass windows and multiple skylights, it had plenty of natural light. The view of the ocean it offered was priceless.

Star was a bit reluctant to give up her cottage though. Jenny had suggested renting it out. It would provide an extra stream of income for Star.

"You will have your own room," Jenny said subtly. "And all the privacy you want."

Star blushed and the ladies laughed. Star had been getting close to a local man. Jimmy Parsons was better known as the town drunk. He had a soft spot for Star. Earlier that summer, he had decided to turn sober. Star had been a good friend to him, providing him the support and understanding he needed. They were not officially dating yet but Jenny knew that day was coming soon.

"The house looks beautiful," Star admitted. "I'm tempted."

"Don't think too much about it," Jenny pleaded. "Nicky won't be here all the time. I need you there."

"You're scared of being there alone, aren't you?" Heather asked, getting up to leave. "I'm off. See you later."

"Why would I be scared?" Jenny asked with a smile.

Heather left without answering her. Molly and Petunia looked uncomfortable.

Star rolled her eyes. "You don't believe in those old rumors, do you?"

"Please!" Jenny groaned. "You too, Molly? You don't really believe the house is haunted?"

"I saw a light flickering there on Halloween when I was 11," Molly said hoarsely. "It was on the top floor."

"Bunch of kids up to no good, I bet," Star said.

She caught Molly's eye and shook her head. Jenny saw the exchange.

"You don't think those old stories are going to spook me, are you?" Jenny asked. "Any abandoned house is bait for this kind of talk. I don't believe any of it."

"Believe what?" an attractive man asked as he came up the steps of the Boardwalk Café.

The cool breeze coming off the ocean ruffled his brown hair. His almond shaped eyes crinkled at the corners as he gave Jenny a wide smile.

Jason Stone was handsome, intelligent and well off. He was the only lawyer in Pelican Cove. He was one of two local men who had a crush on Jenny. Jason had a cheerful, magnanimous personality. He made no secret of the fact that he wanted to date Jenny.

"Have a donut," Jenny offered, hugging him back.

"I'll have two," Jason said, taking a big bite. "So are you ready for the party this weekend?"

"I can't wait," Jenny said eagerly. "Star and I planned the menu."

"You should just order some pizza from Mama Rosa's," Jason told her. "It's your big day. We don't want you slaving in the kitchen."

"Try telling her that!" Star exclaimed.

"What's a party without crab puffs?" Jenny asked. "I have it all under control. And we'll have pizza too, don't worry."

"Will you let me bring the wine?" Jason pleaded. "I did some work for this local winery and they give me a big discount."

"Thanks Jason," Jenny smiled. "I won't worry about the wine then."

Three days later, Jenny's housewarming party was in full swing. Seaview was lit up like a Christmas tree. The contractors had done a great job with the renovation. Jenny loved how they had modernized everything while preserving the best of the original features.

Jenny had decorated the massive great room in a nautical theme.

"The place looks beautiful, Jenny," Adam Hopkins whispered in her ear.

Jenny's heart sped up as she looked at Adam. His blue shirt was the exact shade of his eyes. He seemed relaxed as he leaned on his cane. Adam was a war veteran with a bum leg but he hadn't let it pull him down. He was the sheriff of Pelican Cove, a job which had frequently pitted him against Jenny. Neither could deny the attraction they felt for each other. They had been out on a few dates since summer.

"Mom's done a great job with Seaview, hasn't she?" her son Nick crowed, putting an arm around Jenny's shoulders.

Adam's twin girls handed Jenny a gift wrapped package. They pulled at Nick's arm and were soon out of sight.

"Going after the booze, I bet," Adam snorted.

Luke Stone tipped his glass at Jenny and complimented her. He had been the main force behind the renovation.

"Are you happy with our work, Jenny?"

"Of course!" Jenny nodded. "Cohen Construction has done a fabulous job with the remodel. When am I getting my garden back though?"

Seaview was set on a large ten acre tract. The house itself was surrounded by towering pine trees. It boasted a sprawling garden which had run wild over the years. Gardenias and honeysuckle dotted the grounds and blue wisteria sprawled over the wraparound porch and gazebo. Climbing roses spanned windows and side walls, their heady perfume mingling with the scent of the other blooms.

When Jenny first arrived in Pelican Cove, she had been mesmerized by the roses and the gardenias. It was one of the things that had drawn her to Seaview.

Jenny had been tempted to let the garden run wild. Luke Stone had talked her out of it. He had brought in a landscaper who assured Jenny they would preserve most of the old bushes and trees. There was only one patch of land that needed to be cleared to put in a water feature.

"They are almost done," Luke assured her. "They are working late tonight so they can install that stone fountain tomorrow."

Jason appeared behind Jenny and planted a kiss on her head.

"Congratulations Jenny. May you be happy here for the rest of your days."

Jenny felt a warm glow inside her. Jason always made her feel relaxed.

"Do we have more crab puffs?"

Jenny smiled all the way to the kitchen. Heather was pulling out a tray of warm crab puffs from the oven.

"These are yum!" she exclaimed. "I don't know what I like more, the puffs or that tomato dip."

Molly entered the kitchen, beaming all over.

"Chris likes my dress."

"He's just being kind," Heather dismissed.

"Don't be nasty, Heather," Jenny snapped. She smiled at Molly. "You look pretty tonight."

Molly Henderson was tall and scrawny, with eyes that seemed to pop out of the Coke-bottle glasses covering them. She had begun dating Chris Williams, a local guy who had been Heather's beau until recently.

Adam Hopkins hobbled in just then, wearing a grim expression.

Jenny had a sudden feeling of déjà vu.

"What now?" she whispered.

"It's Luke's men," Adam said curtly. "The ones working in the garden…"

Jenny's eyebrows shot up as she waited for more.

"They found something. I don't know how to say this, Jenny …" Adam hesitated just for a second. "There's a skeleton in your back yard!"

Chapter 2

Jenny stifled a yawn as she mixed muffin batter for breakfast. Her regular customers would be lining up soon to get their morning fix.

The housewarming party had gone downhill after the startling discovery. Adam had taken over in his role as sheriff. Law enforcement had swooped in with their forensic team and secured the area. Jenny and her guests had been asked to leave the premises.

None of her guests had been ready to go home, of course. They had just moved the party next door to Star's cottage. The food and wine had continued to flow as everyone talked about the discovery of the skeleton.

"Why does this always happen to you?" Star had moaned. "I don't want you getting involved in this, Jenny."

"It's my house. I'm already involved."

"You know what I mean?"

Jenny's reputation for amateur sleuthing preceded her. Star had been unjustly accused of a murder a few months ago. Jenny had stepped in to clear her name. Since then, she had been instrumental in solving a few murders in town.

"What's wrong with Pelican Cove?" Heather cried. "The bodies just keep dropping."

"This one dropped a long time ago," Jason commented.

"Did you see it?" Jenny asked eagerly. "Tell us something about it."

Jason had barely noticed the tattered remains of some clothes on the skeleton. He tried to steer Jenny away from the gruesome topic.

"That house has been sitting empty for twenty five years," Betty Sue proclaimed. "Anyone could have been squatting there."

"So you think this was a tramp?" Jenny asked eagerly.

"We won't know more until the police tell us something," Star quipped.

"Adam's not going to tell us much," Jenny said flatly.

Adam Hopkins was never forthcoming with information related to crimes. Jenny had been at loggerheads with him about it several times.

"Good Morning, young lady!" Captain Charlie's voice boomed, snapping Jenny out of her reverie.

Jenny looked up at her favorite customer. Captain Charlie was always the first in line when the Boardwalk Café opened at 6 AM.

"Your usual?" she asked him, pouring coffee and placing a warm muffin on a small plate.

News traveled fast in Pelican Cove.

"What's this I hear?" Captain Charlie asked. "You're like a magnet for dead bodies."

He guffawed at his own joke, then turned serious.

"You be careful now, you hear? Take care of yourself."

"There's nothing to be afraid of, Captain Charlie. Whoever it was died a long time ago."

"This is going to stir up a storm. Mark my words."

Captain Charlie's warning barely registered as locals and tourists thronged the café. Jenny eagerly waited for a chance to take a break.

Betty Sue swooped in a few hours later, her hands busy knitting something purple. Heather followed close behind.

Jenny went out to the deck, carrying an assortment of baked goodies and fresh coffee. Her aunt was already there, talking softly to Petunia.

Molly was engrossed in a book as usual.

"I guess you won't be moving in to your new home now," Betty Sue clucked.

"It might take a couple of days," Jenny agreed. "I'm thinking I will let Luke's men finish the landscaping first."

"But you're still moving in?" Molly asked, looking up from her book.

"Of course I am. What do you mean?"

"You aren't spooked by Mr. Bones?" Heather laughed.

"How do you know it's not Mrs. Bones?" Jenny asked.

The girls found it funny and broke into a giggling fit.

"Stop kidding around, girls," Star grumbled. "This is serious."

"What do you expect me to do?" Jenny demanded. "Shut up Seaview again?"

"Nothing good ever came from living there," Betty Sue warned. "That place is jinxed."

"Don't you mean haunted?" Jenny asked.

"That too," Betty Sue huffed.

"That's it!" Jenny said, banging a fist on the table. "I have had enough of these insinuations. I want to know everything about Seaview. Right now."

"What's the point of that now?" Star asked.

"I am the new owner of Seaview, for better or for worse. I want to know the history of my house."

Star looked at Betty Sue and gave a slight nod. Betty Sue put her knitting down with a sigh and sat back in her chair. She folded her hands and got ready to tell a story.

"Why don't you pour us all a fresh cup of coffee?" Betty Sue asked. "You are going to need it."

Molly bit into her second donut and everyone hunkered down with their food and their drinks.

"You have heard about the Pioneers," Betty Sue began.

The town of Pelican Cove had a peculiar hierarchy. People who had originally moved to Morse Isle with James Morse were called the Pioneers. There were five such families and they considered themselves special. Betty Sue belonged to this coveted group.

"You mean the five Pioneer families?" Jenny nodded.

"Once there were six," Betty Sue explained. "John Davis was the first man to come join my ancestor here on the island. The Davis family flourished on the island. One of their descendants built Seaview."

"I think that name sounds familiar," Jenny agreed. She remembered seeing the name on some legal papers related to Seaview. "So the Davis family lived at Seaview? When was that?"

"The house was built in the 1950s. The family moved in toward the end of that decade."

"You must have been really young then, huh, Grandma?" Heather asked.

"I was a young woman in my teens," Betty Sue dismissed.

"How many people were there in this family?" Jenny asked eagerly.

"Old man Davis and his wife Mary and their two children," Betty Sue told them. "Their daughter Lily was my best friend."

"You had a best friend?" Heather asked, surprised. "But you never talk about her!"

Betty Sue ignored Heather's outburst.

"Their son Roy lived with them. He had a wife and two sons. Alan was four and Ricky was just a baby."

Betty Sue paused and took a deep breath. Her eyes were moist and she had a faraway look in her eyes.

"They were such a happy family," Betty Sue whispered. "A pretty family."

"What happened?" Jenny prompted gently.

"The great storm of 1962," Betty Sue said heavily. "Half the island was washed away. People scrambled for their lives. Some managed to evacuate in time. Some didn't."

"Seaview must have been hit hard, being on the beach," Jenny spoke.

"Old man Davis thought he was invincible," Betty Sue said angrily. "He thought his new house was strong enough to withstand any storm. His overconfidence cost him his life."

There were gasps and exclamations around the table.

"The waves hit strong and hard. Half the house was submerged. The old couple was swept away. Roy died saving little Alan. Roy's wife took the baby up to the third floor. She and Lily watched their family drown in the sea."

"That's horrible," Molly said.

"Didn't anyone try to save them?" Jenny questioned.

She was so engrossed in the story she could almost hear the waves roar.

"There wasn't anyone around to help," Betty Sue explained. "Everyone was trying to save their own lives and their families."

"So your friend lost most of her family in a single day," Petunia clucked.

"Lily was devastated," Betty Sue nodded. "She came to stay with us for a while. I remember she cried for hours, calling for her mother."

"Those poor women!" Star gushed. "What did they do?"

"Roy's wife Ann shut the house up. She was from somewhere in the mountains of North Carolina. She took Lily and the baby with her."

"And Seaview has been abandoned since then?" Jenny asked.

"Do I look like I am done yet?" Betty Sue snapped.

She cleared her throat and tapped her empty cup. Jenny went inside to get a fresh pot of coffee.

"It was the summer of 1989," Betty Sue continued after taking a bracing sip. "Heather was three or four. Her parents were letting her spend the summer with me."

"I vaguely remember going to visit someone," Heather said. "It was in a big house by the sea."

"Lily came back to Pelican Cove that summer," Betty Sue told them. "She was married, with a family of her own. Her son was in college and her daughter had just started high school."

"Why did Lily come back?" Molly asked Betty Sue.

"She said she missed town. Her husband got a job in Virginia Beach. Her kids had grown up hearing about Pelican Cove and Seaview. The kids had never seen the ocean. They were eager to live in a beach community."

"They sound like a normal family," Jenny said.

"They were normal alright," Betty Sue sighed wistfully. "Laughter rang through the halls of Seaview. Lily was the perfect mom, baking cookies for her daughter's friends, volunteering in school activities. Then disaster struck."

"What now?" Jenny cried.

"Lily's daughter died."

"What?" Heather burst out. "You never told me any of this, Grandma."

"What's to tell? You were just a child then. You wouldn't have remembered any of them."

"What happened to the girl?" Jenny interrupted.

"It was some kind of tropical virus. Nobody knew where she got it. Her fever soared overnight. She was gone within hours."

"Poor Lily," Jenny mumbled.

As a mother, she couldn't imagine anything happening to her son. Losing a child was any parent's worst nightmare.

"Lily was devastated," Betty Sue said grimly. "Grief must have turned her head."

"Why? What did she do?"

"Lily ran away."

"What?" Jenny cried out.

"She must have been seeing someone on the sly," Betty Sue reasoned.

"Did you know anything about it, Grandma?" Heather asked. "Wasn't she your best friend?"

Betty Sue looked sad.

"We had grown apart by then. I tried to reach out to

her after her baby girl died. But Lily locked herself in that house. Her husband was at work most of the time. Her son was in college. She barely left the house. I took some food to her a few times. After a while, I just gave up."

"And all this time she was having an affair?" Molly mused.

"We'll never know that," Betty Sue pursed her lips. "Rumor has it, she got into a car one dark night and ran out of town."

"How did her husband take it?"

"He closed up the house and went away. The son never came back either."

"When was this, Betty Sue?" Jenny asked.

"Fall of 1991."

"And you never heard from any of them again?" Heather asked.

Betty Sue shook her head.

"I will never understand why Lily abandoned her family. The Davis name has never been spoken of again in town. Most of the people who settled here after the big storm have never heard of them."

"Now you know why that house is jinxed?" Betty Sue thundered. "None of the locals like to talk about it."

"Why didn't you tell me all this before I bought the house?" Jenny asked curiously.

"You didn't ask," Betty Sue shrugged. "You just announced one fine day that you bought Seaview. I didn't see a point in saying anything after that."

"Say what you will," Jenny said firmly. "I don't believe in superstition. I know the Davises had a string of bad luck. But that's not going to happen to me."

Jenny forced herself to ignore the obvious – the skeleton the men had found in her backyard.

"Hello ladies!" a cheery voice startled them out of their misery. "It's a beautiful day, isn't it?"

Jenny rushed into Jason Stone's arms and hugged him tightly. He made her believe everything was going to be alright.

Chapter 3

Jenny ladled thick pumpkin soup into a bowl and garnished it with toasted pumpkin seeds. She sprinkled a bit of Old Bay seasoning on top. People on the Eastern Shore loved to add it to their food.

Molly buttered the thick crusty bread Jenny had set before her.

"You are in early," Jenny remarked as she served Molly's lunch.

"The library board is meeting today," Molly explained. "It's all hush-hush. The staff was asked to leave the building."

"This gives us a chance to catch up," Jenny smiled. "How's it going with Chris?"

Chris Williams, a thirty something young man, came from a local Pioneer family. He had always been tight with Heather. Their families had been sure they would get engaged soon. Heather had shocked everyone that summer with a different kind of announcement. She wanted to date other people. Chris had matched her step for step by putting up his own profile on the online dating sites. Molly had expressed an interest in going out with Chris.

"We went out a couple of times," Molly said shyly. "Just as friends."

"You think he's just waiting for Heather to go back to him?"

"I don't know, Jenny," Molly muttered.

Molly really liked Chris. She had confessed as much to Jenny. Jenny was afraid Heather and Chris were just playing some kind of game. Molly was going to end up getting hurt.

"Don't get too attached," Jenny warned. She tried to change the subject. "How do you like the soup?"

"It's delicious!" Molly exclaimed. "The tourists are going to love it."

"Petunia says we have more tourists this fall," Jenny said, "thanks to Instagram. They just won't stop coming."

"Good for business, right?" Molly said. "I just wish there was a way tourists could come to the library. We can use the business."

A short, middle aged man entered the café. Jenny guessed he was around fifty. She had never seen him before. His clothes were rumpled and had seen better days. The man came up to the counter.

"Hello!" Jenny greeted the stranger. "Here for some lunch?"

The man looked at the floor and mumbled something.

"How about some pumpkin soup?" Jenny suggested, trying to guess what he had said. "I just made a batch of chicken salad sandwiches."

The man nodded but didn't look up. Jenny brought his order out and pointed to a table near the window.

"How do you do it?" Molly asked, biting into her sandwich. "You are so good with people."

"It's just instinct," Jenny shrugged.

She placed a slice of chocolate cake before Molly and took one to the stranger.

"Care for some dessert?" she asked. "It's on the house."

"Have you moved into your house?" the stranger asked suddenly.

Jenny was speechless. She stared at the man, unable to think of a reply.

"You are the new owner of Seaview, aren't you?" the man asked.

He looked directly at Jenny, his light brown eyes boring into hers.

"Who told you that?"

"It's all over town," the man laughed. "You can't keep a secret in a small town like this."

"Do you live in Pelican Cove?" Jenny asked.

"Oh no! I'm just visiting."

Jenny held out her hand and introduced herself.

"My name is Jenny King. I moved here a few months ago."

"I know who you are," the man nodded, taking a bite of his cake. "Yes Sir!"

"What is your name?" Jenny asked him directly.

"Keith Bennet," the man said softly. "You can call me Keith."

"Nice to meet you, Keith," Jenny said lightly. "So where are you from?"

"Here and there," the man answered evasively.

He shoved another bite of cake into his mouth and spoke with his mouth open.

"Did you know about the skeleton in your backyard?"

"I did not."

"Gave you a shock, I suppose."

"I guess you can say that."

"Are you selling the house? Good luck with that. It's falling apart."

"No it's not," Jenny argued. "I did some extensive renovations. Seaview is ready to be lived in."

"How did you buy the place anyway?" Keith asked. "Didn't anyone tell you the place is jinxed?"

"I don't believe in such nonsense."

"You will," Keith nodded. "Wait and watch."

"Excuse me, are you threatening me?" Jenny cried.

"Nope," Keith said, getting up. "Just telling it like it is. If I were you, I would get rid of it as soon as possible."

"Thanks," Jenny snorted. "I'll think about it."

"What was all that about?" Molly asked. "He sounded like a nutcase."

"He knew a lot about what's happening in town."

"Be careful, Jenny," Molly urged. "Don't talk to strangers."

Jenny put her hands on her hips and glared at Molly.

"What am I, eight? I run a café, Molly. Half the people walking in are strangers. How can I not talk to them?"

"Just be careful then," Molly repeated as she rushed out.

Jenny walked to the police station after the café closed. Nora, the desk clerk, waved her through.

"He's not in a good mood," she warned.

Adam Hopkins had a mercurial temper. His mood swings were frequently brought on by his injured leg. Jenny found him struggling with a bottle of pain pills. She took the bottle from him and unscrewed the top. Adam popped a couple of pills and washed them down with water.

"What do you want, Jenny?" he snapped.

"Thanks for the nice welcome," Jenny smiled back.

"I'm busy."

"Just tell me when I can move into my home."

"It's going to take a while," Adam grunted.

"How long is a while?" Jenny pushed. "A week? Two weeks? A month?"

"I really can't say at this time."

"You know I moved most of my stuff into Seaview. I barely have a few clothes at Star's cottage."

"I can send a deputy with you to the house. Take what you need."

"What I really want is to start living there."

"I know that, but my hands are tied. This is an ongoing investigation."

"What is the urgency? Whoever it was, obviously died a long time ago."

"I'm waiting for the autopsy results."

Jenny sighed and sat back in her chair.

"Do you think the house is jinxed, Adam? That's what everyone is saying."

"Have you lost your mind, Jenny?"

"A guy came in to the café asking all kinds of questions about the house. He even knew about the skeleton."

"Every kid in town knows about it," Adam smirked. "It's front page news in the Pelican Cove Chronicle."

"He seemed suspicious."

"I'm sure," Adam muttered, flicking the pages of a thick file.

"He gave me all kinds of warnings about the house."

Adam looked up and sighed.

"People are talking about Seaview up and down the coast. I'm sure each one of them is going to have some advice for you. Are you going to listen to all of them?"

"You're right," Jenny said, getting up. "Am I seeing you later?"

Adam and Jenny had an unofficial standing date every evening. Jenny loved going for a walk on the beach after dinner. Adam went there with his dog Tank. After running into each other a few times, they began looking forward to it.

"I have an appointment in the city," Adam told her. "I might be late getting in."

Jenny walked out, wondering why Adam made her heart flutter. He was in a grumpy mood most of the time.

Star was sitting on the porch of her cottage. Jimmy Parsons sat with his arm around her. Jenny greeted them when she got home. Her son Nick had gone back to college. She rubbed the tiny gold heart that hung on a chain around her neck. Nick had gifted her a gold charm every Mother's Day since he was eight. Jenny wore all the charms on a chain. They stayed close to her heart, giving her a tangible connection to her only child.

"I am heating some leftovers," Star called out. "Come out when you are ready."

They dined on an assortment of dips and crackers and leftover pizza.

"You'll have to tolerate me some more, Auntie," Jenny joked. "They aren't allowing me to move in yet."

"Don't be silly, child. I never reckoned you were going to buy that mansion next door. You can stay here as long as you want. We are getting along fine, aren't we?"

Jenny stole a glance at Jimmy.

"I don't want to be in the way."

"You're not in the way, Jenny," Jimmy assured her. "And your aunt and I, we're not..." His face turned red as he trailed off.

A car drove up outside.

"That must be Jason," Jenny said, springing up.

Sprinkles and Skeletons

Jason Stone did not come bearing good news.

"You will have to be patient, Jenny," he told her. "They won't be letting you in yet."

Jenny fixed a plate for Jason and they sat out on the porch.

"I'm tired of people telling me the place is jinxed," Jenny grumbled. "I want to move in as soon as possible and prove them wrong."

"All in good time," Jason said. "So you're not scared of going to live there?"

"I'm tougher than that," Jenny said firmly.

She felt a frisson of uncertainty in her heart but she ignored it. She was a strong, modern woman and she needed to prove her mettle.

"I know," Jason said, tucking a strand of hair behind her ear. "That's the girl I'm crazy about."

"Are you trying to butter me up?" Jenny asked slyly. "What do you want, Jason?"

"A date."

"We talked about this," Jenny protested.

Jenny had resigned herself to the lonely life of a

divorced woman after moving to Pelican Cove. She had never imagined that not one but two handsome men would be pursuing her. All the Magnolias teased her relentlessly about it. They were making bets on who Jenny would ultimately choose. After going on a few dates with Adam, Jenny was clearly leaning toward him.

"It's a law society dinner in the city," Jason pleaded. "And I want a smart, sophisticated, intelligent woman to be my date."

"You forgot beautiful," Jenny teased.

"So you'll come?" Jason asked hopefully.

"Just this once," Jenny said reluctantly.

Jason was so nice it was hard to disappoint him.

"I feel bad about this whole Seaview business," Jason apologized. "I never told you the whole story."

"I didn't give you a chance," Jenny argued.

"Yes, but I could have been more upfront about the Davis family."

"Did you know there was a skeleton buried in the garden?" Jenny asked.

"Of course not!"

"Then I don't see what you could have done. I knew how old the property was. Any house that ancient has some rumors attached to it."

"So you aren't repenting you bought the place?"

Jenny paused to consider.

"Not yet. I want to tackle this situation with a positive attitude."

"That's admirable," Jason said. "I'm here to help any way I can."

"I know that, Jason," Jenny smiled. "You're the one person in this town I rely on completely."

Jenny wondered why she couldn't fall in love with Jason. He made her feel safe and protected. She could talk to him about any topic on earth. He was handsome, successful and sensitive. But he didn't make her heart beat wildly. He was the safe harbor she could come home to but he wasn't the storm that would sweep her off her feet.

Jenny walked on the beach, eager to run into Adam. She turned back after a while. The motion detectors set off the lights at Seaview. Jenny smelled the roses and the gardenias and looked up at the imposing mansion. Was she going to be happy there?

Chapter 4

Jenny was surprised to see Adam in the café.

"You're up early," she observed.

"Shift starts at 8. I thought I would get your special omelet for breakfast today. Dinner wasn't great."

"Western omelets on the menu today," Jenny nodded. "With ham and peppers."

Jenny curbed herself until Adam finished eating. She topped up his coffee and looked at him speculatively.

"Any news?"

"I suppose you are referring to the thing we found in your backyard?"

"Heather and Molly are calling it Mr. Bones," she laughed. "Or Mrs. Bones. Can't you tell me anything about it?"

"You wear me down, Jenny," Adam sighed. "I don't want to argue with you this early in the day."

"Then don't," Jenny winked. "Just throw me some scraps."

"It's female," Adam said. "That's all I can tell you for

now."

Jenny sucked in a breath.

"Poor woman," she muttered.

"I have to get going," Adam said. "See you later."

"That's all Adam told you?" Molly asked as she sipped her coffee.

Betty Sue was busy knitting something with bright orange yarn. She grunted without looking up.

"What else?" Star asked.

"Nothing," Jenny wailed. "Who was this woman? Where did she come from? What was she doing here? I have no idea."

"Let the police investigate," Petunia remarked. "It's their job. Although I assume it's going to be very difficult to find out anything."

"We need to do some research."

"We?" Star's eyebrows shot up. "You're not getting involved in this mess, are you?"

"I'm already involved."

"Not really," Star argued. "Whatever it was, happened before you got here. You should stay away from this,

Jenny."

"That's no reason to let a murderer roam free."

"How do you know it was a murder?" Heather asked.

"Why else would someone bury a body in my garden?" Jenny demanded. "Do you really believe that poor woman died naturally?"

The women paused to think and shook their heads.

"You have no leads at all," Molly said. "Where will you begin?"

Jenny looked at Betty Sue.

"Where I always do. By talking to people who were in the area."

Betty Sue looked up and twirled a thread of wool over her needles.

"Why are you staring at me like that, girl?"

"You are always my best source of information, Betty Sue," Jenny smiled. "You have been around for so long, you know almost everything that happened in this region."

"Are you saying I'm old?" Betty Sue roared.

Jenny struggled to find the right words. Betty Sue

laughed at her discomfort.

"I'm just yanking your chain. What do you want to know?"

"Do you remember any missing women?"

Betty Sue shook her head.

"Not in Pelican Cove."

"Do we know how old the skeleton is?" Molly asked.

"Adam didn't say. I'm not sure he knows."

"What's your next step?" Molly wanted to know.

"I'm going to look up some old newspapers," Jenny said. "I'll see you at the library later, Molly."

Jenny walked to the library after the café closed. She settled down in a small cubicle and began looking at old newspapers. She decided to go back ten years at a time. Small town news covered missing cats and local festivals. Jenny saw no mention of any missing persons.

Jenny skipped through the current decade and focused on the first ten years of the Millennium. Her search didn't return anything. She started on the 1990s after that.

"I can't find anything for 1995-1998," she told the girl at the desk.

The girl looked through her records and shook her head.

"Looks like they were misplaced."

"How is that possible?" Jenny asked sharply.

The girl shrank back in fright.

"I don't know. I wasn't working here at that time."

"How can I find out anything for that period?"

"You can try the newspaper offices," the girl suggested. "They have an archives section too."

"How can a library lose stuff?" Jenny complained. "Aren't you supposed to keep everything safe?"

"We moved here from the old building twelve years ago," the girl told her. "They might have been lost at that time."

"You didn't try to replace what you lost?" Jenny grumbled.

"You're the only one who's asked for those records," the girl said. "It's not a priority, I guess."

Jenny gave up arguing with the librarian. She wondered

why Molly wasn't at her desk.

Adam Hopkins leaned back in his chair when Jenny swarmed into his office.

"How can I help you?" he asked with a smile.

Adam was in a rare good mood.

"I need to see the missing person records from 1995 to 1998."

"What's so special about them?"

"I'm doing some research on missing women," Jenny explained. "I went to the library and looked at their archives. They have lost all the data from those three years. I can go to the newspaper offices but it will be better if I can directly look at your records."

"There you go again, Jenny," Adam sighed. "Why are you doing all this?"

"I want to find out who Mrs. Bones is."

"That's my job, not yours."

"Are you going to let me see your files?"

"They must be down in the archives section. I'll have Nora pull them up for you."

"Thanks," Jenny smiled.

"Do you want to grab some dinner at Ethan's?" Adam asked. "He just got a fresh batch of oysters."

"Oyster season is just starting, isn't it?" Jenny asked. "I'm thinking of adding them to the café menu."

"Are we having dinner or not?" Adam asked impatiently.

"I want to go home and change."

"I'll pick you up in an hour," Adam nodded.

Jenny had a smile on her face as she sailed out of the police station. Molly was sitting out on the porch when Jenny got home. She looked worried.

"Molly!" Jenny exclaimed. "What's the matter? Did you have a fight with Chris?"

Molly shook her head.

"Worse. I'm about to be fired."

"Fired from the library?" Jenny exclaimed. "Aren't you the top librarian there? What about that award you won last year?"

"Most Popular Librarian," Molly grimaced. "Yeah. That's not going to help me."

"Tell me the whole story," Jenny said, sitting down

next to Molly.

She placed an arm around Molly's shoulders. Star came out with tall, frosty glasses of sweet tea.

"Start with this. We can move to something stronger after that."

"The library is out of funds," Molly began. "They are cutting jobs."

"Are you sure about that?" Star asked.

"They are being quiet about it. But I know a girl who took the minutes at the library board meeting."

"Don't they get rid of the nonperforming people first?"

Molly nodded.

"That won't be enough. They are going to cut all the jobs that were added in the last five years. That includes me."

"Will they give you a reference?" Jenny asked.

Jenny didn't have a lot of experience when it came to jobs. She had been a housewife all her life. She had recently started helping out at the Boardwalk Café. Although she was fully committed to the café, it wasn't her livelihood.

"I'm not worried about references, Jenny," Molly sighed. "Where will I go?"

"I'm sure there must be plenty of opportunities for someone with your skills and experience."

"Sure," Molly nodded. She had studied library science in college and was very good at what she did. "But all those jobs are in the city. I'm very happy living in Pelican Cove."

"Oh!" Jenny exclaimed. "What about the other towns along the shore?"

"Most libraries are already staffed. Librarians generally don't go job hopping. Once a position is filled, it's for life."

"We'll think of something," Jenny consoled her. "I want you to stop worrying first."

Molly drank her tea and sobbed silently.

"All's not lost yet, sweetie," Star said. "And you're not alone. We are all going to help you through this."

A car drove up to the cottage and honked. Jenny had completely forgotten about her dinner date.

"I'm going to have dinner at Ethan's," she told Molly. "Why don't you come with me?"

Molly glanced at Adam and shook her head.

"I didn't know you had a date, Jenny. I'm so sorry for holding you up."

"No need to apologize," Jenny said. "The more the merrier. Let's go in and clean up."

Molly texted Chris to come meet them at Ethan's Crab Shack. He was already seated at a table by the water when they got there. He sprang up and hugged Molly.

"Don't worry, Molls. We're going to take care of you."

"The library has never cut jobs before," Adam reasoned. "They must be in really bad shape if they are thinking about it."

"Funding's been reduced thrice in the past year," Molly explained.

"Why don't we forget about that for now?" Jenny asked. "Let's eat."

Ethan came over with platters heaped high with crisp, fried oysters, fat coconut shrimp and beer battered fish.

Adam ordered some raw oysters on the shell. Jenny had never tried them before. Adam sprinkled some hot sauce on an oyster, squeezed some lemon juice on it and coaxed Jenny into tasting it.

"You can't live on the Eastern Shore and not like oysters, Jenny," Chris laughed. "They are going to be your next favorite thing after the soft shell crabs."

Chris offered to drive Molly home. Adam drove Jenny to a small, secluded beach a few miles out of town. Moonlight shimmered over the water and big, frothy waves of an incoming high tide battered the shore.

"You don't mind I brought Molly along?" Jenny asked Adam.

"She's lucky to have you," Adam said gently. "So am I. You're a good friend, Jenny."

"I thought we were more than friends," Jenny said boldly.

"I might need some proof of that," Adam whispered in her ear.

Jenny shivered in the crisp fall air and snuggled close to Adam. Adam pulled up outside Star's cottage an hour later. He picked up a file from the back seat and handed it to Jenny.

"This is a surprise," Jenny said as she saw '1995' printed in bold letters on the file.

"Just this once," Adam said. "I'm not sure what you are going to find in there though."

"You might be surprised, Adam."

Jenny thought of what she had already discovered in the course of her research. But she wasn't ready to talk about it yet.

"How far back are you going to look?" Adam asked. "The skeleton could be a hundred years old for all we know."

"Seaview was built in the 1950s," Jenny pointed out. "I don't think Mrs. Bones is older than that."

"What makes you say that?" Adam asked curiously. "Maybe she's been there for centuries."

"I don't think so," Jenny insisted. "Look, I have to assume something for the purpose of my search. I think this happened after the big storm. Most of the land was submerged at that time, right?"

"Do you think the skeleton was washed up here in the storm?" Adam asked. "It could have got buried in the debris?"

"That's possible too," Jenny agreed. "I'm going after the missing women for now."

"What missing women?" Adam asked as Jenny turned around and walked inside.

Star and Jimmy Parsons were watching an old movie.

"Do you know who owned this stretch of land, Jimmy?" she asked. "Before Seaview was built, that is?"

"That's a bit before my time," Jimmy drawled. "But my guess is the Morse family. They owned pretty much everything on the island at one point."

"Why don't you ask Betty Sue tomorrow?" Star suggested.

"I'm going to," Jenny nodded purposefully.

Was Adam right? Had Mrs. Bones been resting there for the past hundred years? Was she the wife of one of Betty Sue's ancestors? Or a concubine?

Jenny settled into a fitful sleep and dreamed of a family of skeletons living at Seaview.

Chapter 5

Betty Sue Morse wiped the sugar glaze off her mouth with a linen napkin. She picked up her knitting and debated going for a second donut.

"My doctor says I need to watch my sugar."

"We do have muffins," Jenny offered. "I use whole wheat flour and brown sugar in the recipe."

"Tell me what you found out at the library."

Molly hadn't turned up for their coffee break. Jenny decided she was afraid to leave her desk. She was torn between telling the girls about the issues in the library and what she had found out.

"I found plenty of missing women."

"What?" Heather, Betty Sue and Star chorused.

Jenny nodded.

"I went as far back as 1955. Believe it or not, plenty of women have been filed as missing from Pelican Cove."

"I assume all of these reports are from 1962 or 1963?" Betty Sue asked.

"How did you know that?"

"Have you forgotten the big storm?" Betty Sue questioned her. "Entire families were displaced. Many poor souls were literally swept away. I bet all those accounts you read about are from that period."

Jenny's shoulders slumped.

"Why did I not think of that?"

"I'm sure there was a flurry of petty crimes around that time," Betty Sue said. "I remember how it was at the time. The town set up some makeshift camps. We offered shelter to anyone who asked for it."

"And these people repaid you by robbing stuff?" Jenny asked, horrified.

"Many houses were lying abandoned. Doors and windows had been blown away. They were wide open for anyone to plunder."

"I can't believe it!" Jenny breathed. "What were the police doing?"

"There were massive rescue efforts up and down the coast. The priority was taking care of the injured and the infirm. Some people were stranded on the barrier islands. It was a hard time for the town."

"Do you think our skeleton might have been washed ashore from somewhere?"

"Wouldn't someone have spotted it?" Heather asked, barely looking up from her phone. She was engrossed in tapping some keys.

"Put that thing down," Betty Sue rasped. "Are you talking to us or what?"

"I can do both, Grandma!" Heather dismissed.

"The Davis family was grieving," Betty Sue explained. "It was just Ann and Lily and the baby. They were gone within a week."

"Could the garden just have grown over Mrs. Bones?" Jenny gasped.

"Say that's what happened," Star mused, "she has to be from around here. I think you are on the right track, Jenny. You should keep looking for missing women."

"Some of these must have been found, right?" Jenny wondered.

"Either that, or they were declared dead," Betty Sue said.

"I am going to reconcile these names against the county records," Jenny decided.

"That sounds like a lot of work," Star said. "Why don't you split it up among us?"

"I'll get Molly's help," Jenny told them. "She knows her way around the library records."

"Where is Molly, by the way?" Heather asked, looking up. "Why isn't she here today?"

Jenny told them about the problems at the library.

"I know funding has been poor," Betty Sue said. "But I had no idea it was this bad. I missed the last meeting when I had that cold."

"You're on the library board?" Jenny asked, surprised. "Why didn't I think of that? You can find out what's really happening, Betty Sue."

"They mailed me the minutes of the meeting," Betty Sue said. She turned to Heather. "Go get them for me, Heather. They are in the roll top desk where I keep my mail."

Heather stood up and started walking out, her eyes still glued to her phone.

"What's wrong with that girl?" Betty Sue cried. "She hasn't stopped looking at that phone ever since she started that Internet dating nonsense."

Petunia went in to get a fresh pot of coffee.

"Were there any refugees living at Seaview?" Jenny asked suddenly. "Surely they had plenty of room?"

"They sure did," Betty Sue nodded. "But Seaview was a house of mourning. Ann Davis was beside herself. She could barely take care of the baby. She lost her husband and young son in a single stroke. Lily was too young to take any decisions by herself. She came to live with us."

"What about after they left? It wouldn't have taken a lot of effort to break a window and get in."

"It was a sitting duck," Betty Sue said with a faraway look in her eyes. "There were so many people who needed a roof over their heads. There were a couple of break-ins. The police interfered. Then the town people kept watch over the house for a while."

"Why would they do that?"

"We take care of our own here," Betty Sue said grimly. "The Davis family was well respected in these parts. The old man was known for his generosity. He had done a lot for the town. No one thought twice about doing something for them."

"Was Ann Davis supposed to come back?"

"People assumed she would return some day. She was a chicken necker. She barely said goodbye to anyone before leaving."

Jenny recognized the term the islanders used for anyone who wasn't born there.

"Lily was your best friend, right? You must have stayed in touch with her."

"We wrote to each other for a while," Betty Sue replied. "She got married after a few years. So did I. I guess we got busy in our lives. Next thing I know, she's back here with a brood of kids."

"There were almost twenty eight years in between," Jenny calculated. "Was the house empty for all that time?"

"Sure was," Betty Sue said.

"Why didn't they rent it out?"

Betty Sue shrugged.

"There were stories. No one wanted to go near the place."

"What about tramps or other transients? No one ever entered that house?"

"I don't know about that," Betty Sue said, shaking her head. "It was the only house on that stretch of beach for years. Nobody went there after dark. Someone built a couple of cottages there in the 80s. That's when people started living on that side of town."

Heather came back, carrying her poodle Tootsie on a leash.

"Don't take her inside, please," Petunia pleaded. "Just make sure she stays on the deck."

"Don't worry, Petunia," Heather assured her. "I'll tie her to this post. She can play in the sand."

Heather handed over an envelope to Betty Sue.

"What does it say, Betty Sue?" Star pressed. "Read it quickly."

Betty Sue peered at the paper in her hand and her face fell.

"Job cuts are coming alright," she told them. "The board has voted to cull all the jobs created in the last five years."

"That affects Molly!" Jenny gasped. "Poor thing. She really wants to stay in Pelican Cove."

"We need to do something about this, Betty Sue," Star said urgently.

"I can't be directly involved, but I'm all for it. What do you have in mind?"

"We need to raise money for the library, of course," Jenny said. "We need to rally the local businesses and ask them to pitch in."

"Sounds like a drop in the ocean," Betty Sue grumbled.

"There is a huge deficit. I don't know how we are ever going to fill it."

"Could you be a bit more optimistic?" Star snapped. "Jenny will think of something."

"You can have a bake sale," Heather said eagerly. "People love your food."

"I don't think a bake sale is going to cut it, Heather," Jenny said thoughtfully. "We need a big fundraiser, something on a grand scale."

"This is not the city," Petunia observed. "People don't have deep pockets."

"We just need to gather more people then," Jenny said resolutely.

"You need to set up a committee," Star said. "That's the first thing we do here when we have a problem."

"Can you make a few posters?" Jenny asked her aunt. "Ask for volunteers for the committee. I'll post them around at a few local places."

Star rummaged in a bag that lay by her feet. She pulled out a sketch pad and a few colored pens.

"I'll get right to it," she said. "Keep talking."

"Heather, why don't you run a search for library fund

raising ideas on that phone of yours?"

"I'm chatting with a new guy," Heather pouted. "I need to fix a date for the weekend."

"Haven't you any shame?" Betty Sue clucked. "This is the fourth first date you are going on this month. Why don't you ever go on a second date?"

"None of them has been worth a second date," Heather sulked.

"Of course they haven't," Betty Sue cried. "You are never going to find someone as good as Chris."

"Not that again!" Heather moaned. "Chris understands why I'm doing this. He has agreed to wait for me."

"You do know Chris and Molly are seeing each other?" Jenny asked incredulously.

"Oh, that!" Heather dismissed. "They are just hanging out."

"Watch out, Heather. You might have to repent at leisure."

"Stop talking like my grandma, Jenny!" Heather complained.

"Molly's a wonderful girl," Betty Sue observed. "I wouldn't be surprised if Chris fell in love with her."

"Chris has loved only one girl since he was in third grade," Heather boasted. "That's me!"

"You are not being very nice, Heather," Petunia said softly. "Your head has turned ever since you started that online dating."

Petunia rarely said much. Everyone was taken aback by her straight talk. Heather huffed and went on tapping the keys on her phone.

"Here you go!" Star said with a flourish. "Do you like any of these?"

"Already?" Jenny exclaimed in delight.

Star had produced three different posters, each of them asking for volunteers for the library committee.

"'Save our Library' ... I like that." Betty Sue bobbed her head.

They haggled over their choice and finally picked one.

"Let's get this photocopied," Jenny said, getting up. "Coming, Heather?"

"What about the lunch rush?" Star asked. "I can stay back and help Petunia."

"Soup's already on," Jenny assured her. "It's creamy chicken with peas. We are making smoked turkey and pesto sandwiches today. The pesto's already made."

"We can take care of the rest," Petunia said. "You go get those copies."

"I'll be back soon," Jenny promised. "I can put these up later this afternoon."

Jenny walked to the Rusty Anchor after the café closed. It was the local watering hole. Everyone in Pelican Cove eventually ended up there for a pint or a game of pool.

"Hey Jenny!" Eddie Cotton, the proprietor and bartender, greeted her.

"Can you put these up for me?" Jenny asked.

Eddie looked at the poster and frowned.

"What's wrong with our library?"

Jenny spotted Chris and Molly at a table. She walked over and showed Molly the poster.

"We are going to take care of this, Molly. You won't be losing your job anytime soon."

Molly seemed to cheer up a bit.

"What's the latest on Mrs. Bones?" Chris asked with a smile.

"Nothing much," Jenny told him. "None of the local women were reported missing."

"You know, Pelican Cove is pretty isolated. We sometimes forget it's an island."

"What do you mean, Chris?"

"What if someone dumped her here? We are just a dot on the map. The perfect place to hide something, or someone."

"You have given me something to think about," Jenny said.

Eddie brought over a pint and Jenny took a big gulp, her thoughts racing with numerous possibilities.

Chapter 6

The library was crowded when Jenny entered. News of the library's troubles had spread like wildfire. Someone started a rumor that the library was closing down. It seemed like everyone had turned up to check out as many books as they could. Bossy mothers pushed kids into line, clutching piles of books. Jenny tapped her foot impatiently as she waited for her turn.

She had finally squeezed time out to do some research. It had been another busy day at the café. She had fried dozens of donuts, baked several trays of muffins and assembled sandwiches until they ran out of all the food. Her feet ached from running around all day. She ignored her fatigue and settled into a small cubicle.

Widening her search to surrounding areas gave Jenny a lot of different results. Her eyes were heavy with sleep but she plodded on, starting at the year 2000 and moving backwards. She finally hit pay dirt. Jenny eagerly noted her findings in a small notebook. Now she needed to tackle Adam.

Adam Hopkins sat with his bum leg propped up on a chair.

"I'm very busy today, Jenny. I don't have time for small talk."

"This could be important," Jenny bristled. "I want information about some missing women."

"Do you think the police department is here to dance to your tune?" Adam barked. "Go away."

"Why don't you pull these files for me?" Jenny asked, writing down some names on a piece of paper.

"I'm doing no such thing," Adam snapped. "You can forget about it."

"What about Mrs. Bones?" Jenny asked, her hands on her hips. "Have you found anything new about her?"

"Your bag of bones is not a priority," Adam drawled. "Other cases have a higher preference."

"What about my house?" Jenny demanded. "If you're not really investigating, why don't you release it to me?"

"We'll be out of there in a day or two," Adam nodded. "You can move in then if you still want to."

"Of course I want to. It's my home."

"It's not your home yet, Jenny," Adam said softly. "You haven't really lived there yet. Maybe you should reconsider."

"What are you saying, Adam?" Jenny asked him.

"Why don't you talk to Chris? You know he's a part-time realtor, right? Put it on the market. You might get a good price."

Jenny's face took on a pinched expression as she listened to Adam.

"I'm not selling Seaview. I don't understand why you should even suggest such a thing."

Adam leaned back in his chair and folded his hands.

"Aren't you even a bit flustered by this skeleton? Any other woman in your position would have wanted to wash her hands off the whole thing."

"I'm not any woman, Sheriff," Jenny said stiffly. "I'm not going to worry about something that happened decades ago."

"You're one of a kind, Jenny King," Adam agreed.

His eyes glinted with admiration as he stared back at Jenny.

"Pelican Cove is my new home, and so is Seaview," Jenny emphasized. "I plan to grow old there. Anyone who wants to be my friend will have to be fine with my living there."

Jenny turned around in a huff and stomped out.

The Magnolias were all dressed warmly. It was an unusually cold fall day. Salty winds whipped across the deck of the Boardwalk Café, overturning salt shakers and displacing paper napkins. But none of the assembled women wanted to give up their priced view and go inside.

Betty Sue gave a shudder as she pulled off an intricate stitch. She clutched a ball of blue wool in her armpit. Heather was glued to her phone. Molly sat staring in the distance, lost in thought. Star and Petunia were talking about pumpkins.

"How was your trip to the library, Jenny?" Betty Sue asked. "Find anything new?"

Jenny looked pleased with herself.

"I did. Nothing much happened between 1965 and 1990. But three women went missing between 1990 and 2000. I have decided to focus on them for now."

"How will you get more information on them?" Molly asked.

"I exhausted everything I could learn from the library," Jenny told them. "I'm guessing the newspaper archives won't have much more to offer."

"What about old police records?" Molly asked.

Jenny rolled her eyes in disgust.

"That sourpuss Adam refused to help me. So I guess I'm on my own."

"We are here to help you," Star said. "Why don't you run the names by us? One of us might know something about these girls."

"I was going to do that anyway," Jenny nodded.

She pulled out a small notebook and began flipping its pages. A loud voice interrupted them and they stared at each other in dismay.

"Yooohoooo …"

A short, plump woman panted up the café stairs, followed by a well dressed man.

"Hello ladies!" Barb Norton sang out. "I knew I would find you all here."

Barb Norton was the local do-gooder. She volunteered for every town festival and local event and always wanted to take charge.

"I saw those flyers you posted all over town, Star," she began. "Why didn't you just pick up the phone and call me?"

"I thought you must be busy working for the harvest festival," Star mumbled.

"Oh, you are right, dear. The harvest festival is taking up a lot of my time at the moment. But the library!"

She took a deep breath as she said that.

"The library is one of our greatest assets. We can't let it close down."

"It's not closing down yet, Barb," Betty Sue thundered. "Not if I have anything to say about it."

"Job cuts are always the first sign," Barb continued. "What's next, eh? I just couldn't take it."

"What brings you here, Barb?" Petunia asked. "Have you tried Jenny's strawberry glazed donuts yet? They are the latest craze."

"Oh, I can't think of food at a time like this," Barb clucked. "I'm here to offer myself for the library committee."

"Thanks Barb," Jenny said earnestly.

She knew the older Magnolias were always a bit brusque with Barb Norton. But the woman meant well. And she had an endless store of energy she often channelized in altruistic tasks.

"I'll put you down as a volunteer."

Barb patted Jenny on the arm and beamed at her.

"That's not going to be enough. The town needs a strong leader to get through this crisis."

"And that's you?" Star snorted.

Barb ignored her and kept talking to Jenny.

"I'm offering my services as chairperson of the Save our Library committee. You don't need to look any further."

"You know every committee votes for the chairperson together," Betty Sue objected. "We haven't even had our first meeting yet."

"That's just a formality," Barb dismissed. "I'm the person most equipped to lead this effort."

"Aren't you always?" Star muttered.

The man who accompanied Barb Norton had been silent all this time. He cleared his throat and looked at her expectantly.

"I haven't forgotten you," she told him. "Like any strong leader, I've taken the initiative and sought expert help."

"Who's your friend, Barb?" Heather asked, looking up from her phone.

She was eyeing the tall, blue eyed stranger with interest.

His brown hair was combed neatly and his khakis and button down shirt were neatly pressed. Jenny decided he was a salesman of some kind.

Heather spotted the ring on the man's finger and her mouth fell in disappointment.

"Ladies, this is Dale. He lives two towns over."

They greeted the man called Dale, waiting for Barb to list his virtues.

"Dale was dubbed Library Savior by his town newspaper," Barb beamed. "He single handedly led a massive fund raising effort to raise thousands of dollars for their library."

Molly looked at the man with interest.

"Are you a librarian?" she asked.

"Oh no," Dale said. "I work at a local car dealership. I just love books. Always have. I believe a library is the heart and soul of any community. It provides the right foundation for raising smart, well informed kids. It educates society and keeps it from stagnating."

"You got that part right," Betty Sue said grudgingly. "What is it you did for raising all that money?"

"Dale has plenty of ideas," Barb butted in. "He's agreed to sit in on our meetings so we can discuss them. When is the first meeting, Jenny?"

"It's up to you, Barb," Jenny said. She grabbed the opportunity to get something off her plate. "You have more experience about these things."

"Don't worry," Barb consoled her. "You'll be a pro at this too, once you have chaired a few committees."

"Do you have any specific ideas for the fund raiser?" Molly asked Dale.

"I do," Dale told her. "But I prefer to give everyone a chance. Let's see what the people in your town come up with first."

"Isn't that idiotic?" Molly burst out after Barb and Dale left. "If he has some suggestions, why not come out with them right now? What's the point in wasting time?"

"He's so full of himself," Heather complained.

She had lost all interest in Dale after spotting his wedding ring.

"Calm down, Molly," Jenny soothed. "He's just milking the situation. Let him. I don't mind giving him credit if he has concrete ideas."

"Forget about Barb for a moment," Heather said. "What are you going to do about those missing women?"

"I'm not sure, Heather. I'm open to ideas."

"Start with the phone book," Star advised. "It's an old fashioned way of finding someone but it still works."

"That's so quaint," Heather scoffed. "I can look them up online right now."

"Do you expect to find their social profiles?" Molly asked Heather. "They are missing, remember?"

"You both have a point," Jenny told them. "I need to determine if they are still missing. I think I am going to track down their families. Go and talk to them."

"I'm up for a road trip any time," Heather whooped. "Now I have to get going. I have a lunch date in Cape Charles."

"Who are you meeting this time?" Jenny asked.

"A gorgeous stud muffin," Heather crowed. "Here. I'll show you his picture."

"Character is more important than looks," Betty Sue preached. "You should know that by now."

"I'd rather have both," Heather said smugly.

She picked up her fancy new handbag and skipped

down the café steps.

"Did she have her bag with her all this time?" Betty Sue asked the ladies, looking bewildered. "Who's going to take Tootsie for her walk?"

"I'll do it, Betty Sue," Molly offered.

"No. You get back to your desk. Don't give anyone a chance to point fingers."

"What's the use? I'm losing my job anyway."

"Don't give up yet, Molly," Star said. "Barb Norton's taken up your cause. She's sure to raise a storm and get you those donations."

Molly looked surprised.

"We might give her a hard time, Molly," Petunia spoke up. "But Barb gets the job done."

Jenny added her two cents.

"She won us that Prettiest Town award, didn't she? Save our Library is in good hands."

Jenny pushed her notebook toward Betty Sue. She didn't want to waste time looking in phone books if there was a quicker way to get that information.

Betty Sue picked up the notebook confidently. "I know

the old Eastern Shore families. Some of them have been here for generations. James Morse, my ancestor, was known to be a very social man. He invited sailors like him from neighboring towns for an annual barbecue."

"So?" Jenny asked hopefully.

Betty Sue peered at the names and shook her head.

"None of these sound familiar."

"I have a stack of old phonebooks," Star told her. "I'll dig them out for you."

"You think one of these women is Mrs. Bones?" Molly asked.

"I hope not, Molly," Jenny sighed. "I hope they were all found long ago and are living happy, healthy lives with their families."

"What are the odds of that?" Molly asked.

None of the women had an answer to that question.

Chapter 7

Jenny dredged fresh slimy oysters in seasoned flour and fried them. She had already made her special tartar sauce.

"These oyster po'boys are going to be a big hit," Petunia said confidently.

"You really think so?"

"Of course. We have all tasted them. They are delicious."

The aroma of the frying oysters wafted through the café and on to the street. There was a sudden influx of customers asking about the day's specials.

Jenny got busy assembling the sandwiches and served them as quickly as she could. She spotted a familiar figure at a small window table, taking a big bite of her sandwich.

"Hello," Jenny said tentatively, going over to greet Keith. "How's it going?"

"Your food is so tasty," Keith Bennet said, giving her a thumbs up. "Almost like my mom's."

"That's the biggest compliment you could give me,"

Jenny beamed. "Does your mother make these a lot?"

"She used to," Keith said, sounding morose. "She left us."

"Oh," Jenny exclaimed. "I'm sorry about that."

"Why should you be sorry?" Keith laughed.

His eyes shone with a strange light and his laughter sounded a bit crazed to Jenny.

"Enjoy your meal," Jenny told him as she topped up his sweet tea.

"Have you moved into your new home?" Keith asked.

"Not yet," Jenny said.

"Good for you."

"I beg your pardon?"

"Seaview's not going to do you any favors."

Jenny ignored him and walked to the next table. There were two big groups of tourists who were tasting the local oysters for the first time. Jenny glowed as they complimented her food. She had cooked multi course gourmet meals for her husband and his rich friends, but they had never taken the time to praise her cooking. Jenny rubbed the heart shaped charm around her neck, thinking about her old life. She had come a long way from the suburban housewife who scrambled to fulfill her husband's slightest whim.

Petunia handed her a slice of carrot cake when she went back to the kitchen.

"That thug ordered this."

"Who, Keith?" Jenny asked. "He's a bit rough around the edges, huh?"

Keith was sucking his tea through a straw, making a gurgling noise.

"I hear you turned the top floor into a studio?" he called out to Jenny.

"What?"

"Those skylights are cool, aren't they? And the view from those windows is priceless."

"How do you know that?" Jenny asked in alarm.

Keith shrugged and attacked his carrot cake.

"Have you been inside Seaview?" she pressed.

"I'd say that," Keith shrugged.

"How? When?"

Jenny looked at Keith's scruffy beard and noticed the slight tremor in his hands. She pictured him sneaking into her house, touching everything.

"It was a while ago."

"How is that possible? Seaview has been locked up for several years."

Keith scratched his beard and looked a bit uncertain.

"Let's say I managed, okay?"

Jenny put her hands on her hips and glared at him.

"Did you break into Seaview, Keith?"

"Didn't need to," Keith said with a mouth full of cake.

"What does that mean?"

Keith looked over his shoulder and leaned toward Jenny. "I had a key."

"Did the realtor give you one?"

Keith shook his head.

"I used to live there."

"What?"

Jenny collapsed in a chair and stared at Keith.

"Who are you, really?"

"My grandpa planted that garden at Seaview," Keith told her. "He chose every detail, right from the wainscoting to the drapes at the windows. Didn't live to enjoy it though, poor guy."

"You are related to old man Davis?" Jenny asked, her eyes round with surprise.

"Yes Ma'am."

"You're Lily's son," Jenny said in a rush as she connected the dots.

"Guilty as charged!"

"What are you doing in Pelican Cove?"

Keith looked around the café meaningfully.

"Enjoying my summer, like everyone else."

"Do you come here often?" Jenny asked curiously.

Keith shook his head. "I've always wanted to visit. But I never made it back, until now."

"How long is your vacation?" Jenny asked.

"It's kinda open ended. I don't need to rush anywhere."

"Would you like a tour of Seaview?" Jenny asked generously. "The police should let me move in any day now."

"About that …" Keith muttered. He rubbed his eyes and frowned. "Seaview belongs to me, actually."

"You mean Seaview will always be home for you?" Jenny quizzed.

"No. I mean it's my house. I own Seaview."

Jenny laughed.

"Nice try."

"What's so funny? Seaview belongs to me."

"I bought Seaview with a big chunk of money," Jenny said gently. "My lawyer did all the paperwork. I am the legal owner of the house now."

Keith shook his head.

"That's where you are wrong. As a direct descendant of Grandpa Davis, I have an equal right to the property. I am part owner of Seaview. And I didn't give permission to sell."

"I don't know about that," Jenny said, beginning to lose her cool. "There's a piece of paper that says I am the new owner. Seaview is my home now and no one is going to take it from me."

Keith was equally agitated.

"But I didn't give permission to sell."

"Maybe you should see a lawyer," Jenny bristled.

She pulled out a small notepad from her pocket and scribbled Jason's name on it.

"Here's my lawyer's information. Feel free to discuss this with him."

Keith's face had settled into a pout.

"I didn't say they could sell," he repeated. "I'm an heir too. I have rights."

"Goodbye, Keith," Jenny said, getting up.

"I don't like lawyers," Keith mumbled, reading the piece of paper Jenny had slapped on the desk.

He struggled to his feet and shuffled out of the café. Jenny stood staring at his back until he was out of sight. She was trying hard to keep her chin up. Seaview seemed to present a new problem every day. Jenny was beginning to believe the place was jinxed.

Barb Norton came in with Dale. They ordered the oyster po'boys.

"Jenny here has put our town on the map," Barb boasted. "It's October, but the tourist season is still going strong."

Jenny blushed furiously as Dale gave her an admiring look. She sensed he was a bit of a player. He looked very handsome in a blue shirt and neatly pressed khakis. Like Heather, Jenny noticed his wedding band and sighed.

"Does your wife like to read?" she asked politely.

"Our whole family loves books," Dale gushed. "My wife and I read to our girls since they were babies. My youngest started reading at three."

"Is that why you started lobbying for the library?"

"I believe in giving back," Dale said a tad pompously. "The library has given us so much. I want every family like ours to utilize the same benefits."

"Dale and I went through some of the fund raising suggestions," Barb interrupted.

She needed to be the center of attention all the time.

"Oh yeah," Jenny said. "I'm sorry I missed the first meeting. I couldn't get away."

"If you have any input, you can give it to me now," Barb conceded. "I'll make an allowance for you this time, since you started this whole effort."

"You're the expert, Barb. I'm sure you will choose the best option. Just put me to work when the time comes."

Barb narrowed her eyes and questioned Jenny.

"What do you think about setting up a concession stand outside the library?"

"Is that going to be enough?" Jenny asked doubtfully.

"You will just be selling food to the people that come to the main event," Barb explained. "Every little bit helps."

"I need to talk to Petunia about this," Jenny considered. "But I think we can do it at cost. We will donate any profit we make to the library fund."

"That's great," Barb beamed. "Now let me taste these oysters the whole town is raving about."

She took a bite of her sandwich and moaned in delight.

"Charge double for this," she ordered. "It's for a good cause."

Petunia came out and handed her a basket.

"Delivery for the police station."

"Good," Jenny said. "I need to talk to Adam anyway."

"I packed your lunch in there too," Petunia smiled. "Don't rush back."

Adam Hopkins rummaged through the basket and pulled out two sandwiches. He offered one to Jenny.

"Care to have lunch with me?"

Jenny sat down with a sigh. Her feet ached and she had a blister which was beginning to hurt a lot.

"Delicious!" Adam pronounced as he bit into his po'boy. "This sauce is the real deal, Jenny."

"Do you know the family that lived at Seaview?"

"Barely," Adam told her. "The girl was much younger. The boy went to our high school for a semester. Didn't really hang out with him."

"He's here and he's giving me a hard time."

"Who is?" Adam asked with a frown.

He unwrapped two giant cookies and bit into one.

"Keith! Remember I told you about him?"

"You mean the guy you were complaining about two days ago?"

"He says he owns Seaview."

"That's ridiculous," Adam said. "Didn't Jason handle your deal? I'm sure he checked all the boxes."

"I have full confidence in Jason," Jenny said. "But I have a feeling Keith is going to be a nuisance."

"Maybe he just wants to see his old house."

"I offered him a tour. But I guess he wants more."

"More what? Money?"

"He looks quite uncouth," Jenny said. "You should bring him in."

"For what? He hasn't done anything wrong ... yet."

"You don't agree he's suspicious?"

"Where do you meet these people, Jenny?" Adam grumbled. "I think you go looking for trouble."

"He just walked into the café one day. How am I to know he's the prodigal son?"

"You're giving him too much importance."

"He calls himself the heir of old man Davis."

"So he is."

"That doesn't mean he can threaten me."

"Has he really threatened you??" Adam asked patiently. "We might have some grounds to bring him in if he has."

"Not really," Jenny admitted. "He just keeps talking about Seaview."

"Ignore him."

"That's what I plan to do," Jenny said meekly.

Secretly, she decided to give Keith a piece of her mind. Then she realized she had no idea where he was staying.

"Did you go to the Save our Library committee meeting?" she asked Adam.

"Is that the latest of Barb's projects?" Adam laughed.

"Laugh all you want. Molly's about to lose her job."

Adam sobered at the thought.

"Those ladies are always up to something," he explained. "Sign me up as a volunteer. I will help any way I can. But no frivolous meetings."

"When can I have my house back?" Jenny asked next.

"I was saving the best for dessert," Adam smiled.

He pulled open a drawer and took a key from it. He handed it to Jenny.

"All yours, Madam. You can move in whenever you want."

"I hope you didn't mess up the place too much?"

"It could do with a cleaning," Adam grimaced. "I can pitch in."

"We need an army of people to clean a house that size," Jenny sighed.

Jenny felt exhausted just thinking about it.

"Let's meet there at six," Adam suggested.

"It's been a long day," Jenny yawned. "I guess the cleaning can wait till tomorrow."

"Weren't you badgering me all this time about getting that house back?" Adam asked. "Just meet me there at six. And don't worry about dinner."

Jenny walked back home, grumbling about how unromantic Adam was. A group of people greeted her at Star's cottage. Heather, Molly, Chris, Jason and Star stood around, armed with buckets, mops and cleaning supplies.

"Let's get this party started," Star cried.

Seaview sparkled like a jewel a few hours later. Jenny sat on the carpet in the great room downstairs, eating pizza with her friends.

"Welcome home, Jenny," Adam said softly, feeding her a slice of pizza.

He was just a different kind of romantic.

Chapter 8

"How are you settling in?" Betty Sue asked Jenny, her hands busy knitting something new.

"It's a bit different from Star's cottage," Jenny admitted, "but we're loving it."

"We sure are!" Star exclaimed.

She hadn't moved all her stuff into Seaview yet but she had been living there with Jenny.

"I might give in and rent out my cottage after all."

"No suspicious sounds at night?" Heather needled. "Weird lights?"

"None, thank you," Jenny said lightly.

"You can be honest with us," Heather persisted. "Are you saying you aren't afraid at all? Not even a tiny bit?"

Jenny rubbed the tiny horseshoe hanging around her neck.

"I've been so tired, I'm out like a light. And Star's there to keep me company."

"Is Nick coming this weekend?" Petunia asked with a smile.

She had grown fond of Jenny's son.

"Oh yes," Jenny said with a smile. "He can't wait. He's struggling through his mid-terms but he'll be here soon."

"Has Adam visited you there yet?" Heather asked with a wink. "What does he think of your room?"

Jenny's ears turned red.

"How's your love life, Heather?" she shot back. "Been on any dates recently"?

"I bet she's lost count," Betty Sue snapped.

Jenny heard a shout and saw Molly waving at them from the boardwalk. Heather and Jenny watched mystified as she scrambled over the café steps.

"What's the matter, Molls?" Heather asked while Molly caught her breath.

"Haven't you heard?" Molly panted. "It's all over town."

"Sit down, girl," Betty Sue ordered. "Get her some water, Jenny."

Jenny obliged and went in to get some water.

Molly's face was blotchy from the exertion. She

dabbed at it with a paper napkin and drained the glass of water Jenny offered her.

"Someone died."

"Who?" all the women screamed in unison.

"Anyone we know?" Betty Sue asked with a quiver.

Molly shook her head in denial.

"Must be a tourist, I think."

"How did you find out?" Star asked. "We've been here for a while but we didn't hear anything."

"It's Mrs. Daft," Molly explained. "That nosy old lady who is my neighbor. She's been renting her spare room by the week."

"Serves her right," Betty Sue muttered. "She should have thought twice before taking a stranger into her home."

Jenny suppressed a giggle. Betty Sue ran the Bayview Inn. She took strangers into her home every day.

"No, no," Molly corrected her. "The woman is fine. And it's not a room in her house. It's a room over her garage."

"You're not making sense, Molls," Heather said,

tapping some keys on her phone.

"She rented the room to a tourist," Molly began again. "Some guy. They found him dead this morning. An ambulance arrived along with some cop cars just as I was leaving for work. I know because it's right across the street."

"What happened to the poor guy?" Star asked.

Molly shrugged. "No idea."

A familiar voice called out to them from the boardwalk.

"Yooohooo …"

Barb Norton came up the steps, dragging Dale behind her.

"Good Morning," she greeted them. "I think we have it. Dale's come up with the best fund raising idea."

The Magnolias smiled at her politely. None of them mentioned the dead man.

"What about all the ideas we suggested at the committee meeting?" Star demanded. "Didn't any of them meet with your approval?"

"There were some really good ideas," Dale said. "But they are not scalable. Barb told me the amount you need to raise. It's quite a challenge."

"Are we just supposed to accept what he came up with?" Star persisted.

"We are having another meeting of the Save our Library Committee," Barb said patiently. "Dale will have a presentation ready. He's really good at those."

"The people of Pelican Cove can decide if my idea is worthy enough," Dale added.

"That's really kind of you, Dale," Jenny said with a smile.

She could see Heather shaking with laughter, her back to them.

"Dale has been a Godsend for the library in his town. They are working on an expansion plan as we speak. I'm hoping he can work the same magic for us."

"We look forward to the meeting, Barb," Star said grudgingly.

"I have to get back to work," Dale said. "I took a few hours off this morning. Guess who's working late tonight?"

The ladies held off until Barb was out of sight.

"Where does she find these people?" Heather said with

a laugh.

"Forget Barb Norton," Betty Sue said impatiently. "We need to find out more about this dead man."

"How do you propose we do that, Betty Sue?" Star asked.

"Send Jenny to the police station," Betty Sue beamed. "Talk to that young man of yours, Jenny."

"Have you met Adam?" Jenny asked with a roll of her eyes. "He's not going to tell me jack. He'll puff up like a balloon and tell me to stop getting into police business."

"So what?" Heather asked impishly. "You manage to get around him every time."

Petunia cleared her throat and widened her eyes. The ladies hadn't noticed the man who was standing beside them on the deck, leaning on his cane.

"Adam!" Jenny exclaimed. "What brings you here?"

"An early lunch," he said, glowering at Heather. "I need to go into the city."

"Does it have anything to do with that dead man?" Betty Sue asked.

Adam sighed.

"Yes, Betty Sue. And I can't tell you anything else."

"Why not?" she thundered. "We have a right to know what's happening in our town."

Jenny came to Adam's rescue.

"Let's go get your lunch."

Adam followed Jenny into the café.

"What will you have?" she asked him. "Oyster po'boy or the Autumn Chicken Salad Sandwich?"

"I'll go with the chicken today," Adam told her.

His eyes had circles under their eyes. Jenny surmised he hadn't slept well. Adam didn't like being dependent on pain pills. Sometimes he chose to bear the pain. It took a visible toll on his body.

"Are you doing your exercises like the therapist told you?" Jenny asked.

"Stop treating me like a child, Jenny," he snapped.

"You know your leg starts hurting if you skip the exercises," Jenny persisted.

"Do you want to announce my private business to the whole world?" Adam yelled at her.

Jenny took a step back and held up her hands.

"No need to be nasty."

She packed Adam's sandwich in a small bag and added a large cup of coffee. She tossed in two packets of cookies and a muffin, just in case he wanted a snack later.

"Can you tell me who died?" she asked, handing over the bag.

Adam struggled with his answer.

"We haven't released any information yet. The news is already spreading through town though."

"Is it going to stop the tourists from coming here?"

"I don't think so."

"Molly said the man was a tourist. Won't it put a damper on business?"

"He wasn't your regular tourist," Adam said reluctantly. "More like a drifter."

"What's his name?" Jenny asked. "Have you seen him around?"

Adam tapped his foot impatiently and leaned forward.

"You know him," he said. "We found a wallet with his driver's license and a couple of credit cards. His name was Keith Bennet."

"Keith?" Jenny exclaimed. "What happened to him?"

"Can't say yet," Adam said, tight lipped. "You're the only person I know who talked to him."

He pulled out his phone and started tapping on it. He thrust it in Jenny's face.

"That's the guy, right?"

Jenny realized she was looking at a dead body. She shrank back involuntarily.

"That's him," she said with a gulp.

"I have to get going," Adam said. "I guess you'll be talking to the ladies about this."

"Drive safe," Jenny called out after him. "Don't forget your pills."

Jenny's feet wobbled a bit as she went out on the deck. The Magnolias were getting ready to leave.

"Hold on a minute, Betty Sue."

"What's the matter, sweetie?" Star asked with concern.

"Are you feeling alright?" Petunia clucked.

"I'm fine," Jenny assured them. "It's that dead guy. I

found out who he is. Or was."

"Who?" Five voices chorused.

"Keith Bennet. He came to the café a couple of times. I talked to him."

"You poor girl," Star said, stroking Jenny's back. "Did he seem ill?"

Jenny shook her head and swallowed a lump. She looked at Betty Sue, uncertain how to break the news.

"He was Lily's son."

Betty Sue sat down with a thud.

"Lily's son? I didn't know he was in town. What was he doing here?"

"Who's Lily again?" Heather asked.

She had put her phone down on the table for once.

"Lily Davis," Molly reminded her. "Betty Sue's best friend?"

"Oh!" Heather nodded. "That dame who abandoned her kids and ran away."

"That's the one," Betty Sue said stonily.

Molly pinched Heather and shut her up before she said

anything more.

"What was he doing here?" Betty Sue asked Jenny.

"He said he was taking a vacation. He always wanted to come back here."

"Why after all these years?" Molly asked.

"I think it had something to do with Seaview," Jenny confessed. "He kept asking me all kinds of questions about the house."

"He must be nostalgic," Star said.

"I offered to take him there," Jenny told them. "He warned me. He told me the place was jinxed. Nothing good would come from living there."

"That old crap?" Star asked, incensed. "How dare he!"

"He called himself the heir. Said he had a stake in Seaview."

"But you bought the place, didn't you?" Petunia asked with a frown. "Did he really own the house?"

Jenny shook her head.

"I have proof. And Jason did the paperwork. Keith was just trying to make trouble."

"He won't be doing any more of that, poor guy,"

Molly said.

"What about his family?" Betty Sue asked hopefully. "Did he say where he lived? Did he mention his mother?"

"He did," Jenny nodded. "He told me she was a great cook."

"Oh," Betty Sue murmured. She seemed disappointed. "Lily created magic in the kitchen. Just like you, Jenny."

"Let's go, Grandma," Heather urged. "I need to do some housekeeping before that couple checks in later today."

"Tootsie must be hungry," Betty Sue said suddenly.

She dropped her knitting in her bag and struggled to her feet. Her face had turned ashen. Jenny felt worried about her.

"How about some lemonade before you go, Betty Sue?" she asked. "Just a couple of sips?"

"I'm fine, girl!" Betty Sue's voice trembled. "I've buried more loved ones than I can remember."

Star stayed behind, assuring Jenny she wasn't busy. Jenny and Petunia worked in tandem and assembled a platter of chicken sandwiches. Jenny started frying oysters.

"The hungry hordes will be here soon," Petunia chirped. "Do we have enough cookies for dessert?"

Jenny nodded as she transferred a basket full of crispy oysters to a paper lined tray.

"What happened to that guy?" Star asked Jenny. "How did he die?"

"Adam didn't say."

"Seems kind of suspicious, huh?"

"You think so?" Jenny asked, whirling around to face her aunt. "He was about my age, I guess."

"A healthy young man," Star repeated. "Did he look ill?"

Jenny thought for a moment while she dredged a bunch of oysters.

"Not really. But he looked scruffy. He wasn't normal."

"Poor guy," Star sighed. "What else did he say to you?"

"He told me his grandpa planted our garden," Jenny said sadly.

"Luke's men are setting up the fountain today," Star reminded her. "Are you going home early?"

"I want to," Jenny said hesitantly.

"Why don't you go on then?" Star said. "Petunia and I can take care of the lunch crowd."

"Eat before you go, Jenny," Petunia told her.

Jenny sat at the small kitchen table and took a bite of her chicken sandwich. A single thought nagged her as she remembered the photo Adam had shown her. Why had Keith really come to Pelican Cove?

Chapter 9

Jason Stone sat in his office, working through a big stack of files. Jenny knocked on his door tentatively.

"Can I come in?"

Jason's face lit up.

"Jenny! Please say you are here to save me from this."

"You need to get a paralegal," Jenny told him. "Or a secretary at least."

"I want to manage on my own as much as I can," Jason explained. "Never mind that. You're a sight for sore eyes."

"This is not a social call," Jenny warned him.

"How can I help you?" Jason asked seriously.

"Did you hear about the dead man?"

"I heard some buzz," he nodded. "But I don't know much."

"Do you remember Keith? Lily's son?"

"Keith Bennet? Vaguely. Why?"

"It was him."

Jason's eyebrows shot up.

"What are you saying, Jenny? The dead guy was Keith Bennet? What was he doing here in town? And how do you know him?"

"He was here on vacation."

"Again, how do you know that?"

"He came to the café a couple of times," Jenny told him. "We talked."

"He's been absconding for a long time."

"He kept talking about Seaview and his grandpa – old man Davis. Said he was an heir and Seaview belonged to him."

"You have nothing to worry about," Jason assured her. "You own it clear. No one can ask you to leave."

"I told him that," Jenny nodded. "I even offered to let him look around."

"How did he die?"

"You'll have to ask Adam. He's not volunteering any information."

Jason opened a small refrigerator tucked in an alcove

and pulled out two bottles of juice. He offered one to Jenny.

"So Keith Bennet comes back to Pelican Cove after twenty five years and now he's gone. It's almost as if he came here to die."

"I had the same thought," Jenny said glumly. "He warned me about Seaview. Said nothing good would come of living there."

"Wait. You don't seriously believe that?"

"I moved in, didn't I?"

"That doesn't answer my question."

"I don't know, Jason. A lot of bad things happened in that house."

"That was a long time ago."

"What about Keith?"

"You don't even know how he died. I think you're letting the talk get to you."

"What did you mean earlier when you said he was absconding?"

"Keith was right about being an heir," Jason sighed. "Roy and Lily were the old man's direct descendants.

Their kids were next in line to inherit. That's Ricky and Keith."

"So Keith didn't know Seaview we being sold?"

"Ann Davis was listed as the sole owner. When you expressed an interest in the house, I tracked her down. She told me Keith had an equal stake in the house."

"That was nice of her."

"I thought so too," Jason agreed. "We tried to track Keith down. It seems he didn't stick around in one place for long."

"He doesn't have a family?"

"Lily's husband, his father, is still alive. He's in a senior home in Texas."

"How did you convince Ann?"

"Ricky tried to track Keith down. We even placed an ad in the paper, asking him to get in touch. But like I said, he was nowhere to be found."

"He must have got wind of it somehow."

"I guess," Jason speculated. "Ann told me she would split the money with Keith whenever he turned up."

"Maybe he didn't want to sell," Jenny mused. "It

sounded like he had an emotional attachment to the house."

"He had plenty of time to come back here and live at Seaview," Jason said, shaking his head. "For whatever reason, he chose not to. You shouldn't worry about it, Jenny."

"I need to get a dress for that law dinner," Jenny said, changing the subject.

"You look beautiful in anything," Jason said sincerely.

"I don't want people to talk behind your back. I know how those dinners work. The women gossip about who was wearing what for weeks after."

"Let them," Jason said loyally. "I care about you, sweet Jenny, not some catty women I may never meet again."

Jenny had a smile on her face as she walked to the seafood market. Jason always made her happy.

Chris Williams was stacking some cans when Jenny walked in.

"Hey Jenny," he greeted her. "Got a minute?"

"Sure, Chris. What's on your mind?"

A troubled expression flitted over his face.

"I am thinking of taking Molly to the Steakhouse."

The Steakhouse was the only formal restaurant in Pelican Cove. It was reserved for special occasions. Jenny realized Chris was taking a big step.

"Do you think she is ready?" he asked.

Molly had confessed her feelings to Jenny a few weeks ago. She had admired Chris from a distance ever since high school. She had been infatuated with him for a long time. Jenny was sure Molly was ready to date Chris seriously.

"I think so, Chris," Jenny smiled. "When are you going to ask her?"

Chris rubbed his hands and looked uncertain.

"Tonight. I hope she doesn't say no. This will be our first official date."

"What about Heather?" Jenny asked shrewdly.

"What about her?" Chris shrugged. "Heather and I will always be friends. But I need to get on with my life. Molly and I click. Who would've thunk, huh?"

"You are all dear to me, Chris," Jenny said sincerely. "All three of you. I hope you find the happiness you deserve."

Jenny grilled fish and tossed a salad for dinner. The kitchen at Seaview had been completely renovated. Jenny had double ovens and granite countertops with a large center island for doing her prep.

"Do you want to sit out on the patio?" Star asked. "It's a bit chilly out there."

Jenny opted to eat inside. The patio had a clear view of the spot where they had found Mrs. Bones. Jenny found she wasn't ready to sit out there yet.

Jenny chatted with her aunt for some time and then stepped out for her walk. She hadn't talked to Adam all day and she was hoping to run into him. She saw him in the distance, throwing a stick for his dog Tank. Tank abandoned the stick as soon as he spotted Jenny and ran toward her.

"Hello darling!" Jenny crooned as the yellow Labrador put his paws on her shoulders.

Jenny scratched Tank below his ears and waited for Adam to walk up to her.

"Hi Jenny," he greeted her. "How was dinner in your new home?"

"Different," she admitted. "The kitchen is huge! Takes some getting used to."

Adam took Jenny's hand and started walking away

from Seaview. Tank walked beside them, wagging his tail.

"Why don't we go on a trip somewhere?" he asked her.

"We can go check out the fall foliage," Jenny offered. "The twins were raving about it."

"The Shenandoah Valley is a three hour drive from here. That's six hours to and fro. We might have to stay over."

"Or we can start really early and spend the whole day there," Jenny quipped.

"You don't think we are ready for an overnight trip?" Adam asked hoarsely.

Jenny's heart fluttered at the innuendo.

"Let's start small," she blushed.

"I didn't mean … that is …" Adam muttered. He was beginning to look alarmed. "There's no rush, Jenny. I don't plan to let you go anytime soon."

Jenny giggled and snuggled into Adam's arms.

The Boardwalk Café was packed to the gills the next day. Jenny had produced a few batches of pumpkin spice donuts in the spirit of the season. They had sold before the glaze dried. She hadn't been able to taste a single one.

The Magnolias breezed in at their usual time. The Eastern Shore weather often produced warm days in October. The sun shone brightly and they sat on the deck, drinking coffee and eating warm banana nut muffins with a special cream cheese spread.

"Jenny cooked her first meal at Seaview," Star told the girls. "It was delicious."

"We need a spa night," Heather declared, peering at her toes. "What do you think, Molly?"

Molly was looking quite chipper. Jenny shared a smile with her. It looked like Chris had already talked to her about their date.

"Spa night sounds great, Heather," Jenny said. "I need to glam up before this party I have to go to."

"Adam's taking you to a party?" Star asked.

"No, Jason. It's work related."

Betty Sue looked up from her knitting and narrowed her eyes.

"What's that Hopkins boy doing on the beach?"

Adam Hopkins strode across the boardwalk, flanked by two deputies. He limped up the café steps and cleared his throat.

"You need to come with me, Jenny."

Jenny stared back at the man in uniform. He looked and acted like a stranger.

"Where are we going?" she asked, bewildered.

"You are a person of interest in the murder of Keith Bennet. I am taking you in for questioning."

"What nonsense!" Star cried.

"You just had to call, Adam," Jenny said. "I would have come over myself."

"Please come with us now," Adam said firmly.

He took Jenny by the arm and pulled her to her feet.

"No need to manhandle her, boy!" Betty Sue boomed.

"Calm down, everyone," Jenny urged.

Her eyes were frantic with worry.

"Go get Jason," she told Heather.

Adam walked down the steps with Jenny in tow.

"What's wrong with that boy?" Petunia groaned. "I thought he was going out with our Jenny."

"He doesn't have his priorities right," Star spat.

"Adam's a bit of a jerk," Molly agreed. "How dare he treat Jenny like that."

Heather hung up her phone and interrupted Molly.

"Jason's in court. He won't be back until later today."

"What do we do now?" Star asked with a frown. "Is he going to lock my Jenny up?"

"Let's all go to the police station," Betty Sue said grimly. "We will wear him down."

"You don't think we are going to scare Adam, do you?" Molly asked. "What if he arrests us all."

"I want to see him try!"

"Calm down, Grandma," Heather warned Betty Sue. "You need to watch your blood pressure."

"Hush, Heather," Betty Sue shushed her.

She looked at Star and Petunia. The two older women got the signal and stood up. They hurried down the steps to the boardwalk.

"Wait!" Molly called after them. "I'm coming with you too."

Heather's phone dinged just then and she began

tapping keys on her phone.

The women were panting and sweating by the time they descended on the police station. Betty Sue's face looked like a ripe tomato.

"Where is she?" Star yelled. "Where's my Jenny"?

Nora, the desk clerk, pointed at a closed door.

"With the boss. Ya'll will have to wait outside."

The women started talking at once. A door banged and Adam came out, looking furious.

"What's all this ruckus?" he demanded.

"Have you arrested my Jenny?" Star shot back. "We have come to rescue her."

"Jenny's fine," Adam sighed. "She's answering a few questions. You can wait for her here if you promise to be quiet."

"I want to see her," Star insisted.

Adam peeked into the small room and said something. Jenny came out and waved at them.

"Where's Jason?"

"Jason won't be back until later today," Molly explained. "You're on your own until then."

"I'll be fine, I guess," Jenny said uncertainly. "It's not like I killed the man."

She glared at Adam Hopkins before she went back into the room.

"You're so busted!" Molly told Adam.

Adam leaned on his stick and limped back into the room.

The ladies sat down and waited impatiently for Jenny. It took a while for the facts to sink in.

Betty Sue voiced the question everyone wanted an answer to.

"Who killed Lily's boy?"

Chapter 10

"I hope you gave that boy a piece of his mind," Betty Sue fumed.

She had still not forgiven Adam for the way he treated Jenny. Jenny herself wasn't feeling too kindly toward Adam. But she assumed he needed to do his job.

"He's very particular about his duties as the sheriff," she said diplomatically.

"Bah!" Betty Sue exclaimed. "He's too full of himself, you mean."

"Have you met Jason yet?" Heather asked.

"I'm going to," Jenny said. "In fact, I'm leaving right now."

"Jason's the better man," Star butted in. She clearly preferred Jason over Adam. "I hope you don't find that out the hard way, Jenny."

Jenny didn't take the bait. She walked to Jason's office. He had come in late the previous night. He didn't know much about the drama that had unfolded.

Unlike Adam, Jason had a quirky sense of humor. But he could be serious when needed. He cut to the chase.

"Does Adam think you are a suspect?"

"He called me a person of interest, but that's just mumbo jumbo."

"What exactly did he ask you, Jenny?"

Jenny gave an account of her conversation at the police station.

"Do you know why he thinks you are involved?"

"I talked to Keith a couple of times," Jenny shrugged. "Apparently, I'm the only person in town to do that."

"That doesn't make sense. Surely he did other stuff? He must have gone to the pub, or grabbed dinner somewhere."

"How much trouble am I in, Jason? Do I need to rustle up bail money?"

"I hope not," Jason said in a steely voice. "You know Adam. He likes to act first and think later. I'm going to talk to him."

"So looks like someone had it in for Keith," Jenny mused. "Will you contact his family?"

"I already passed on that information to the police," Jason said. "I doubt he'll be missed. His father's memory failed long ago. Ann and Ricky are his only living relatives as far as I know."

"Poor guy," Jenny breathed. "I want to find out what happened to him, Jason."

"I strongly advise against that," Jason warned. "You are already involved. Don't make things worse for yourself."

"You said it," Jenny argued. "I'm involved anyway. The only way I can clear myself is by finding the person who did it."

"Where are you going to start?" Jason asked, folding his arms and leaning back in his chair. "What do you know about Keith Bennet?"

"You are going to help me," Jenny said sweetly. "Can't you have someone run a background check?"

"You want me to hire an investigator so you can play Nancy Drew? Isn't that a bit much?"

"We just need to know about his past," Jenny said firmly. "Like where he lived before he came here. Did he work somewhere? Was he married? Stuff like that."

"And that's going to be enough for you?"

Jenny smiled coyly.

"It's a start."

Sprinkles and Skeletons

Jenny picked up Heather at the Bayview Inn that evening.

"Do we have to go?" she groaned. "I just want to put my feet up and watch a movie."

"You started this whole thing," Heather teased.

"I didn't," Jenny shook her head. "I don't know where Barb got the idea."

"You took the initiative and made those posters, didn't you? Barb's your big fan now. She's going around telling everyone how you're almost a native now."

The Save our Library committee was meeting at the town hall. The older ladies had saved them some seats. Star patted an empty one beside her when she saw Jenny. Barb eyed her and lunged toward Jenny.

"Your place is right here, up on the stage."

"Oh Barb. I couldn't."

"Take credit where it's due. You're the driving force behind this effort."

Heather grinned mischievously.

"What did I tell you?" she mouthed.

Dale sat on the stage next to Jenny. He was wearing a

suit and tie.

"They are going to be blown away," he told Jenny.

Clearly, he wasn't lacking in confidence.

The lights dimmed and Dale stood up to start his presentation. Jenny had to admit he did a good job. The idea he presented was new to her. She wasn't sure how well it would work.

"Sounds like tommyrot to me," Betty Sue spoke up. "So someone pays me money to read a book? Why can't they just put the money in a drop box?"

"A read-a-thon is much more than that," Dale hastened to explain. "You are achieving several objectives at once. You nurture a love for reading among your population, young or old. People donate money to encourage that and also to further your cause."

"Let the people speak for themselves, Betty Sue," Barb Norton called out. "You can cast your vote like everyone else."

"Did that stuff make any sense to you?" Star asked Jenny as they waited at Mama Rosa's for their pizza.

"A bit," Jenny said with a frown. "People will donate money for a certain number of pages read, or hours. And they will also donate in terms of effort. And the best part is they can do both."

"There's a limit to how much people will shell out. That's why we have a funding issue in the first place."

"Don't forget the tourists," Jenny reminded her aunt. "Petunia said we are having an unprecedented season this year. The hayrides and the autumn fair will draw in more people."

"Why would a tourist care about our library?"

"Why does a donor care about anything?" Jenny asked. "They are just being charitable."

"What about the prizes that Dale guy mentioned?"

"We'll find out when the time comes."

Jenny was glad for the motion detectors at Seaview. The grounds lit up before they went in. Jenny settled into her couch and took a big bite of pizza.

"Why isn't Jimmy here?" she asked her aunt.

Jimmy Parsons hadn't made an appearance since they moved into Seaview.

"He's out of town," Star told her. "Should be back tomorrow."

"What's he doing out of town?"

"No idea," Star said with a shrug.

Aunt and niece ate their dinner and talked about mundane things. Jenny tried on the new dress which had arrived by special delivery. She looked like her old self in the mirror. But she had come a long way from being a bored and ignored wife.

Jason's eyes gleamed with admiration as he held the car door open for Jenny. Jenny enjoyed the heated seats and swanky sound system in the luxury car. Jason played her favorite blues hits and Jenny forgot about Keith Bennet for a while.

Jenny was happy to see she didn't stick out like a sore thumb at the law society dinner. She struck up a conversation with an attractive young brunette in the ladies room.

"You are one lucky woman," the girl crooned. "If I had a guy like him, I would hold on to him for life."

"Jason and I aren't married," Jenny hastened to explain. "We are just friends."

"Then you don't mind if I make a move?" the girl asked brashly.

"Aren't you here with someone?"

"My douche of a date stood me up. Didn't go down well with my partners, I can tell you."

"You're a lawyer?" Jenny asked.

"I handle divorce," the girl nodded. "These dinners can get pretty boring. Your man is like a breath of fresh air."

Jenny felt uncomfortable in the brazen girl's company. She muttered goodbye and turned to leave.

"Oh by the way, I'm Kandy," the girl said. "Kandy with a K."

"Pleased to meet you," Jenny said politely.

Jason was deep in conversation with a bunch of suits. Jenny waited for him at the bar. Kandy cornered Jason the moment he started walking toward Jenny. Jason smiled politely and made small talk with the girl. Jenny knew he would never be rude.

"That is one aggressive woman," she said when Jason finally joined her.

"Kandy? She seemed sweet."

Jenny was tense as she baked a batch of muffins at the café. Adam hadn't talked to her since he had whisked her to the station. He seemed to have forgotten everything about their trip.

Molly rushed in when Jenny was chatting with Captain Charlie.

"Molly! It's barely 6 AM. What are you doing here so early?"

Molly widened her eyes and tipped her neck at Captain Charlie.

"I couldn't sleep. How about some coffee, Jenny?"

"Have a good day, ladies!" Captain Charlie smiled and walked out with his coffee and muffin.

"Wait till you hear this, Jenny. Let's go in."

Jenny took Molly out on the deck. The early morning chill made her shiver. There wasn't a single soul on the beach that morning.

"You remember Mrs. Daft?" Molly asked urgently. "My neighbor?"

"You mean the woman who rented her room to Keith?" Jenny asked.

Molly nodded eagerly.

"Look what she found!"

She pulled a chain out of her pocket and dangled it before Jenny.

"Does this belong to Keith?"

"She cleaned the room after the police handed it over

to her. This was lying in a dresser drawer."

"How could the police not find it?"

"I don't know," Molly said impatiently. "Do you want to look at it or not?"

"How many people have rented that room this year, Molly?" Jenny asked with her hands on her hips.

"I don't know. Plenty, I guess."

"How do you know this belongs to Keith then? It could have been there forever if it was that well hidden."

"Or Keith hid it really well for a reason."

"Is it gold?"

"I doubt it," Molly said, eyeing the chain.

It was tarnished beyond recognition. It was hard to say if it had been gold or silver once.

"So it's not valuable?" Jenny asked with a sigh. "Looks like a piece of junk to me."

Molly's face fell.

"It might have sentimental value."

Jenny put the chain in her apron pocket.

"We can look at it later. I have to go."

The line of people waiting for coffee stretched out to the sidewalk. Jenny apologized and offered a free muffin to the first ten people in the line.

The Magnolias arrived one by one. Jenny got off her feet and dug into a muffin. She was dreaming about getting a day off.

"So?" Molly asked as she hurried up to the deck from the boardwalk. "Did you show it to them?"

"I almost forgot," Jenny said.

She pulled out the chain from her pocket and put it on the table.

"Molly's neighbor found this. We don't know if it belonged to Keith."

"Have you checked inside?" Betty Sue asked, picking up the chain.

"Huh?" Jenny asked.

Betty Sue pressed some point and the locket sprang open.

"These kind of lockets were very popular when I was a young woman," she told them.

"There are two pictures inside," Betty Sue said, squinting her eyes.

Her eyes filled up as she peered at the photos.

"This is Lily's boy alright. He was one good looking fella."

Jenny thought about how unkempt Keith Bennet had been. He had lost his looks along with his youth.

"Hand it over, Betty Sue," Star ordered. "I might remember the boy."

"There's a girl's picture here," Betty Sue said, holding on to the locket. "But she doesn't look like Lily's girl."

"She must have been his girlfriend," Heather giggled.

The locket was passed around the table. Everyone looked at the photos and made some comment. Jenny snapped a few pictures of the locket and the photos with her cell phone.

"You're sure this is Keith?" she asked Betty Sue. "This belongs with the police. I have to turn it in. You better come with me, Molly."

Chapter 11

Jenny stifled a yawn as she dipped hot donuts in glaze.

"You look worn out," Petunia said sympathetically.

"You work as much as I do," Jenny observed. "But you always look fresh as a peach."

"Go on now," Petunia blushed. "No need to flatter me. You forget I've been doing this for twenty five years. I am used to it. And you've taken most of the work off my hands."

"I can't imagine taking care of the café alone," Jenny said honestly.

"Take a day off," Petunia pressed. "Why don't you youngsters do something fun? Go on a picnic or something."

Heather and Molly wholeheartedly embraced the idea of a picnic.

"Let me call Chris," Heather said.

"He loves the idea," Molly said before Heather could place the call. "He just texted me. He knows the perfect place."

"Are you going to invite Adam?" Heather asked Jenny.

"He hasn't spoken to me in a while," Jenny said. "He might give me a wide berth until the case is solved."

"That's ridiculous," Star said. "What if the case is never solved?"

"Keith deserves better than that."

"You barely knew the guy, Jenny," Heather said with a smirk. "How do you know what he deserved?"

"Surely no one deserves to be killed in cold blood?"

"How goes the search for the missing women?" Betty Sue asked.

"I've barely had any time to work on that," Jenny admitted. "I made a few calls using the phone book. I tracked down a couple of women on the list. One of them was found dead later. It seems she took her life."

"How sad," Molly sighed.

"One of them came back a couple of years later. So she's not missing anymore."

"Where was she for a couple of years?" Heather asked.

"I didn't ask," Jenny said. "I am thinking she needed a time out."

The older women exchanged knowing looks at that.

"How many more names do you have on the list?" Star asked. "You want me to make some calls when I get home?"

"Would you?" Jenny asked. "That will be a big help."

"So you've got a long way to go before we find out who Mrs. Bones is," Heather noted.

"There's a family in the next town. Their young girl went missing some years ago. I want to go talk to them."

"Just say when," Heather said. "You know I'm your wingman."

"Wing woman," Molly corrected her. "Or wing person."

"Whatever, Molls!" Heather snapped. "Who cares!"

Jenny hoped she wasn't around when Heather found out about Molly's date at the Steakhouse.

Two days later, the girls were piling into a big SUV. Chris was at the wheel. Heather was about to climb into the front seat when Chris held her off.

"Why don't you come on front, Molls?"

Molly nudged Heather aside and sat next to Chris. Jenny placed a big wicker basket on the back seat and patted the space next to it.

"Come on Heather, we're getting late."

"I hope we have enough food," Jenny said.

"Don't worry," Chris assured her. "There's a great restaurant overlooking the beach. We are going there for lunch."

"I thought this was a picnic," Heather pouted. "Aren't we supposed to sit on blankets and eat something from that basket?"

"We'll do that too," Chris consoled her. "Okay?"

"I hope you don't feel outnumbered," Molly murmured to Chris.

"We might even out the numbers later," Chris said cryptically.

Chris drove at a leisurely pace, and they passed signs for several small towns. Chris regaled them with stories about houses he had sold in those towns. He made a turn about an hour later and drove down a single lane road. The trees grew dense and formed a canopy over their heads. They came upon a cluster of homes and Chris pulled up in front of a corner house.

"Where are we?" the girls cried. "Aren't we going to the beach?"

"Patience, ladies!" Chris smiled.

He produced a key to the house and led them inside.

"This one just came on the market. I have the owner's permission to hang out here any time I want to."

"Sounds like a generous fellow," Jenny said graciously.

Chris rushed them through a foyer and a large great room. He flung open a set of wide doors leading on to the deck.

There was a collective gasp of surprise.

The deck ended on a white sandy beach. The blue waters of the Chesapeake Bay stretched out before them, the gentle waves lapping against the shore.

Chris pointed to a building in the distance.

"That's one of the best restaurants in these parts. We can walk there through the sand."

He turned toward Heather.

"And you can have your picnic on the beach wherever you want."

Heather was going around, clicking pictures on her

phone.

"Is this the best place or what?"

Jenny had collapsed into a large armchair and put her feet up on an ottoman. The blue waters filled her vision and she sighed with pleasure.

"I'm not moving from here."

Chris and Molly picked a small couch next to Jenny. They followed her example and sat down. Chris put an arm around Molly and they shared a special smile.

Heather watched them with a curious expression.

"Don't tell me Molly's getting all lovey dovey."

"You need to tell her," Molly told Chris.

"Tell me what?"

"We went to the Steakhouse a couple of nights ago."

"Why? It's not like you're serious about each other."

Molly and Chris stared back at Heather. Jenny cleared her throat. A range of emotions flitted across Heather's face as she finally caught up.

"Molly's your girlfriend now?" she asked Chris. "Your actual girlfriend?"

"I am so grateful to you, Heather," Chris said earnestly. "If you hadn't tried that online dating business, I would never have gone out with Molly. We connect on a different level."

"I thought we had a connection, Chris," Heather said.

Jenny sensed the desperation in her voice and felt sorry for her. Chris and Heather had been together since third grade after all.

"It's different with Molly. Something you and I never had."

"Really?" Heather barely whispered.

Molly's eyes were full of adoration as she stared at Chris. She was completely oblivious to Heather's shocked expression.

Heather started pulling things out of the basket. She unwrapped a muffin and bit into it. She picked up another container and spoke to them with her mouth full.

"I'm starving. I'm eating this on the beach."

She sped down the stairs to the sand and went out of their line of vision.

"That went well," Jenny drawled.

"She'll be fine," Chris said lightly. "Heather likes to make a scene."

"Should I go check on her?" Molly asked seriously.

"No need. You are not going to feel bad about this." Chris placed both hands on Molly's cheeks and stared into her eyes. "Remember what we talked about, Molls. We have done nothing wrong."

Molly nodded. The couple embraced and Jenny found herself tearing up. All the Magnolias had warned Heather against taking Chris for granted. It looked like she was going to learn a bitter lesson. Jenny felt happy for Molly though. Molly was a victim of domestic violence. Her past had made her shy and docile. Jenny believed Chris was going to be the perfect companion for her.

Footsteps sounded on the deck and Jenny felt her pulse speed up. Adam Hopkins strode up, his eyes hidden behind dark glasses.

"Adam!" Chris smiled. "You made it."

"I started my shift early. It's a beautiful day. I didn't want to miss it."

Jenny turned her back on Adam and leaned back in her chair. She slipped on her sunglasses and pretended to stare at the water.

"Hello Jenny," Adam said tentatively, taking a seat beside her. "How are you?"

"I'm good," Jenny said tersely. "I was having a great time until now."

"Do you want me to leave?"

"I don't want you to do anything, Adam."

"You're still mad at me."

"Gee Adam, why would I be mad at you? What have you done?"

"Jenny, please, don't be like this."

"Like what?"

"You know I have a job to do. I take my duties seriously."

"I can understand that," Jenny scowled. "Did I say a single word when you carried me away like a common criminal? I didn't. Because I know you were just doing your job. Of course, there's more than one way to do your job. But let's not go there. Let's consider being nasty and rude is part of your job description."

"Jeez Jenny, take a breath."

"I don't have any problems with you doing your job,

Sheriff. But where have you been since then? I haven't seen a glimpse of you these last few days."

"I've been busy at work," Adam said lamely. "Can't you forgive me, Jenny?"

"I'll think about it."

Molly was looking over the stuff in the basket.

"I'm starving. Are we going to eat this or go to the restaurant?"

"Let's finish this first," Chris said. "We can have an early dinner at the restaurant."

Jenny munched a piece of fried chicken and stared moodily at the water. Adam's presence had disturbed her equilibrium. She wasn't sure if she wanted to talk to him or give him the cold shoulder.

"How are things at the library?" Adam asked Molly.

"I am expecting to get my two week notice any time now."

"Aren't they planning some kind of fund raiser?"

"It might be too little too late. But Betty Sue is trying to convince the board to hold off for a while."

"She gets her way more often than not," Adam said

kindly. "We might have some staff positions coming up at the department."

"It's not what I am trained for but I will take anything at this stage," Molly said seriously. "Thanks Adam."

There was a flurry of footsteps on the deck and Jenny turned around to see who the latest arrival was.

Jason Stone strode in with his hands in his pockets. He was dressed casually in chinos and an open collared shirt. A sweater was tied loosely around his shoulders. An attractive brunette followed him on the deck and beamed at Jenny.

"Surprise!" she shrieked.

"Cindy, right?" Jenny asked.

"No. Kandy, with a K. We met at the law society dinner?"

"Oh yeah, right … what are you doing here?"

"Jason and I met in court. He told me about this picnic on the beach."

"You came at the right time," Chris told her. "We just started eating."

Heather had come up from the beach while they were talking. Kandy regaled them with her exploits in court.

She had everyone in splits. Chris and Jason found some logs stacked at one side of the deck. They built a fire as the sun went down.

Jason pulled out a can of soda from a cooler and offered it to Jenny.

"Thanks for introducing me to her. She makes me feel alive, Jenny."

"You're welcome," Jenny grunted, ignoring the pang of regret she felt inside.

"Why are you digging around in Keith Bennet's background?" Adam asked Jason.

"I'm not doing anything illegal."

"You are meddling in my investigation, Jason."

"Not true," Jason said firmly. "I'm just looking out for my client."

Adam whirled toward Jenny.

"Are you getting him to do your dirty work now?"

"Someone's gotta do it," Jenny quipped.

"When are you going to leave things alone?" Adam asked, exasperated. "Did you even know the guy?"

"If you believe Jenny didn't know the guy," Jason

asked, "why are you treating her like a suspect?"

"Anyone who talked to him is a suspect," Adam shot back.

"Jenny had nothing to do with Keith's death," Jason growled. "You would believe that too if you were her true friend."

"Of course I'm her friend," Adam cried.

"Prove it," Jason seethed as he turned his back on Adam.

Chapter 12

Adam planned a day trip for him and Jenny.

"How about going this Sunday?" he asked.

"I just took a day off," Jenny told him coldly. "I can't just take off again."

"The foliage cam shows peak color at this time. Pretty soon, there won't be any fall colors left to see."

"There's always next year," Jenny said with a shrug.

Adam picked up his coffee and muffin and left the café without a word. Jenny wondered if she was being too hard on him. But she couldn't forget the humiliation he had put her through.

She went to Jason's office after the café closed. Jason sat with his feet on the table, talking to someone on the phone. He pointed at the chair, inviting Jenny to sit down. He burst into laughter a couple of times before he hung up.

"That Kandy," he said with a shake of his head. "She's a hoot."

His eyes shone with admiration.

"Looks like you two hit it off."

"You know how stodgy lawyers can be, Jenny. Kandy's a breath of fresh air. She's always ready with a smile."

Jason offered a bottle of water to Jenny and took one himself. He gulped a few mouthfuls before he spoke.

"I'm glad you came. I was going to call you anyway."

"Did you find something?" Jenny asked eagerly.

"A can of worms," Jason sighed. "Keith had a long history of drug abuse. He barely kept down a job. He was supposed to be in a rehab facility a few years ago. But we don't know if he was still sober."

"How did he get here?"

"He must have felt strongly about Seaview."

"That was obvious, I guess."

"There's more," Jason said. "He had a police record."

"Surely Adam knows about this?" Jenny asked, incensed.

"He must have run a background check, just like we did," Jason nodded.

"What was his crime?"

"Possession of drugs. My guess is he was a small time drug dealer."

Jenny sucked in a breath.

"That sounds dangerous."

"He owed money to some baddies. One of them might have followed him here."

"So he was killed for money?"

"Money, drugs, revenge – it's anybody's guess."

"What do the police say about this?"

"I was about to go talk to Adam when you came in."

"I'm coming with you."

"Let's go," Jason nodded, standing up.

Jenny noticed he didn't put an arm around her shoulders like usual.

"He's in a mood," Nora, the desk clerk, warned Jenny as they knocked on Adam's door.

Adam Hopkins sat with his leg propped up on a chair.

"What do you want?" he barked at Jenny.

"We want to share some information," Jason said,

following her inside.

He gave Adam a brief version of what he had told Jenny.

"Believe it or not, we are aware of all this," Adam shot back.

"Does that mean Jenny is no longer a suspect?"

"I didn't say that," Adam said sharply.

"You have plenty of suspects who had a better motive than Jenny here," Jason argued.

"But none of those people are here in town as far as we know. They didn't have the opportunity."

"And Jenny did?"

"She's the only person we know of so far who talked to the man."

"That doesn't make her a killer."

"Imagine the number of people who could have had it in for Keith," Jason exclaimed. "Fellow junkies, dealers, loan sharks … the list is endless."

"Once again, Jason, are any of them here in town?"

"I don't think anyone would follow Keith all the way to Pelican Cove just for a bit of money."

"Thank you for your input," Adam said sarcastically. "Can I get back to work now?"

"What about his family?" Jenny asked, ignoring Adam's barb. "This aunt and cousin Jason told me about? Did they get along with him?"

"Tell me you don't suspect the Davis family, Jenny?" Jason asked.

"Why not? If I can be a suspect, why not them?"

Jason didn't have an answer for that.

"Do you have the autopsy report yet?" he asked Adam. "Surely you can share it with us?"

"He died from an overdose," Adam told them.

"Could it be suicide?" Jason asked right away.

Adam didn't care to elaborate.

"You have a lot of leads to pursue," Jason hinted.

"And I can't do that until you leave," Adam said curtly.

Jenny turned around without a word and stomped out.

"What's wrong with you, man?" Jason asked as he followed her out.

Star cooked dinner for them that evening. Jimmy

Parsons was back in town and he had come over.

"You have done a great job with this place, Jenny," he complimented her. "What measures are you taking for security?"

"This is Pelican Cove, Jimmy," Star reminded him. "We don't even lock our doors here."

"Motion sensing lights come on if anyone gets close," Jenny told him. "I think that's good enough."

Seaview had always had those. For the first time, Jenny wondered why.

"You're brave," Jimmy said with a shrug. "Two women on their own in this big house."

"Two poor, helpless women?" Jenny smirked. "We can take care of ourselves if needed."

Truth be told, Jenny wasn't sure what she would do if anyone attacked them.

"I have lived right next door all these years, Jimmy. All by myself. Stop trying to scare us."

Jenny stepped out for her walk an hour later. The roses and gardenias perfumed the air with their heady fragrance. Jenny stood in the garden, reveling in the salty breeze coming off the ocean.

Her feet ached but she forced herself to walk a mile. Part of her hoped she would run into Adam. She wanted to give him a piece of her mind. But Adam and Tank were nowhere to be seen.

Jenny pulled out her third batch of banana walnut muffins out of the oven. She was making mushroom soup for lunch. Heather came in to the kitchen, looking somber.

"What's on your mind, honey?" Jenny asked immediately.

There was a temporary lull in the café. Jenny made sure everyone who was seated had what they wanted. She poured fresh coffee in two mugs and placed two muffins and a crock of butter on a plate.

"Let's go sit outside."

"Take your time," Petunia whispered to her. "Something's not right with that girl. I can feel it."

Heather barely waited for Jenny to sit down.

"Did you see how they were carrying on?" she cried. "Right in front of me too."

Jenny steeled herself for a difficult conversation.

"This is too much," Heather muttered, crumbling the muffin with her fingers. "I can't take it anymore."

"Are you talking about Molly and Chris?" Jenny asked gently.

Heather's look of despair was answer enough.

"They are serious about each other," Jenny said simply. "I think they might even have a future."

"What about my future with Chris?"

"You were the one who chose to date other people."

"Are you going to rub it in? Chris has always been there for me. Always. I trusted him."

"This is a difficult situation, Heather. You created it. Please don't ask me to judge who's right or wrong. I can't."

"What am I going to do, Jenny? I love him. How can I bear seeing him with another woman, someone who is my friend, no less."

"You'll have to suck it up. I'm sorry, sweetie. Life hands us tough breaks sometimes."

"So I just put on a smile and pretend nothing has changed?"

"Something like that."

"What if I talk to Chris? Beg him to take me back?"

Jenny took Heather's hands in hers. She could feel Heather's pain.

"I think that ship has sailed," she said reluctantly. "At least for now."

"So you think they might not make it?"

"I don't think any such thing, Heather. I can't. You are all my friends and you have come to mean a lot to me. I want you all to be happy."

"What about my grandma?" Heather asked, her eyes filling with fear. "She won't take it well."

"We'll have to break it to her gently," Jenny nodded. "But I wouldn't worry about her."

"I was always supposed to marry Chris," Heather said with a faraway look in her eyes. "I dug my own grave."

Jenny sat with Heather for a long time, trying to pacify her as much as she could. Heather finally broke down. Tears streamed down her eyes and nothing Jenny said could console her.

Heather left before it was time for the Magnolias to come in.

"Where's Heather?" Molly asked.

"She's taking Tootsie for a walk," Jenny told them.

"Tootsie had her walk in the morning," Betty Sue said sharply, looking up from her knitting. "What's that girl up to now?"

"Let me guess," Molly chirped. "She's on a date."

Molly was glowing with happiness. Her bright orange tunic suited her well. Jenny thought she looked pretty.

"What's the latest on the Save our Library project?" Star asked. "Has Barb assigned tasks to the volunteers yet?"

"We need readers," Jenny told them. "People who can read fast and read a lot."

"Everyone reads. What's the big thing about it?"

"The more people read, the more money we can raise," Molly said. "Will I be allowed to volunteer?"

"I don't see why not," Betty Sue declared. "We all need to pitch in if we want to save the library. I am going to put my name in and ask the other board members to do the same."

"So the board is not against this fund raising effort?" Star asked.

"They better not be," Betty Sue grunted.

A uniformed guy walked up the steps with a big

bouquet of red roses.

"Delivery for Jenny King," he said.

The women exclaimed over the flowers and peered over Jenny's shoulder as she read the attached card.

A blush stole over her face and she smiled broadly.

"They are from Adam."

"That boy has finally done something right!" Betty Sue exclaimed. "What does he say?"

"He wants to take me to dinner tonight."

"Will you go?" Molly raised an eyebrow.

"Of course I will," Jenny gurgled.

"You're too easy," Star snorted. "I would make him squirm a bit."

"He says he's sorry," Jenny reasoned. "That's good enough for me."

"We should go on a double date," Molly beamed.

Betty Sue narrowed her eyes.

"Since when do you have a young man, Molly?"

Molly reddened and looked at Jenny. Jenny gave her a

shrug. Molly gulped before answering Betty Sue.

"I have an announcement. Chris and I are seeing each other."

This was news to the older ladies. Star and Petunia congratulated her warmly. Everyone waited for Betty Sue's reaction.

"You're a good girl, Molly. I know you'll treat him better than my Heather did."

"What are you doing later?" Jenny asked her aunt. "Can you make some phone calls for me?"

"Bring them on," Star said with a nod. "Jimmy and I will do it together."

"Any updates on Mrs. Bones?" Molly asked.

"The police are tight lipped as usual. I'm going to have to ramp up my own efforts."

"You're seeing Adam tonight," Star reminded her.

"That's personal," Jenny said quickly. "Adam is very particular about keeping his professional life separate from his private one."

"What a fusspot," Star grumbled.

"He's a stickler for doing the right thing," Jenny

defended him. "I like that about him."

"What else do you like?" Petunia winked. "Those baby blue eyes of his?"

Jenny let them tease her. She was busy thinking about what to wear for her date. She didn't know what Adam had planned for the evening. Would he take her to the Steakhouse?

Chapter 13

Barb Norton had taken over the conversation as usual. The Magnolias were not happy. Betty Sue drained her coffee and focused on her knitting. Star doodled something on a paper napkin. Heather was engrossed in her phone and Molly sat staring at the ocean with a smile on her face.

"Are you listening to me, Jenny?" Barb asked sharply. "What do you think?"

"I agree," Jenny nodded. She forced herself to concentrate on Barb. "So you are saying we should ask people to pay for one hour segments?"

"Donate, Jenny, donate," Barb corrected her. "We need to use the right lingo."

"I still don't get it," Star grumbled. "How much will people donate for one hour?" She stressed the word donate.

"We spread the event over three days," Barb said. "We can set up a marquee in the town square. All the readers will sit there and read as much as they can. They will report every hour that is read. One of the moderators will keep track of the hours."

"Go on," Star said, waving a pencil in the air.

"The donors will give money by the hour. So for example, one man might donate money for five hours. The moderator will deduct those hours by five."

"How much will they donate?" Jenny asked.

"We are giving them three options," Barb explained. "We want to keep it simple. So we have $5, $25 or $50. This way they can choose the hourly rate and the number of hours and pay according to that."

"So a man choosing five hours at $50 per hour pays two fifty." Star did the math.

"Exactly!" Barb beamed.

"Is this really going to work?" Jenny asked. "Do you think people will donate that kind of money?"

"They will," Dale spoke up.

He had been leaning against a pillar, listening to them.

"Most people will donate both money and time. You will see."

"I need some food photos from you," Barb told Jenny. "Those donuts you are making look good. We need to put them all over that Internet."

She looked at Heather with a frown.

"Can I count on you to spread the word online?"

"Sure, Barb," Heather said without looking up.

"People will want to make a day of it," Barb said with a gleam in her eyes. "How can we make this better? Think!"

"What about offering a hayride on the beach?" Star asked. "It's the right season. Food, fun, books and a chance to do something for a good cause … sounds like a day of fun to me."

Barb didn't leave them until she had discussed the finer points of the proposed read-a-thon. Jenny was beginning to look forward to it.

Adam came to the café for lunch. Jenny had a special smile for him as she served him his tomato soup. Jenny's wish had come true. Adam had taken her to the Steakhouse and treated her like a queen. Jenny was beginning to discover a different side of Adam. She just wasn't sure when his pleasant persona would disappear and he would start berating her. It was almost as if he had two personalities.

"What are you doing later?" he asked as he took a hefty bite of his oyster po'boy.

Jenny thought of the little excursion she had planned with Heather. Adam was better off not knowing about it.

"Just some girl stuff with Heather," she smiled.

Jenny felt apprehensive as she piled into her car that afternoon.

"Did you feed the address in your phone?" she asked Heather.

"It's pretty straightforward, Jenny. Take the bridge out of town and turn right on the state road. Then you have to make a left after ten miles."

"Do you think they'll talk to us?"

Heather shrugged. "We don't even know if these are the right people. Did you just ask them about the missing girl?"

"Their daughter," Jenny supplied. "Star talked to them. I don't know how she tackled them."

"They agreed to meet you, right?" Heather reasoned. "What's the worst that could happen?"

"They'll turn us out," Jenny quipped. "You're right. I'm just a bit nervous."

"This is so not like you."

Jenny fingered the tiny gold charm around her neck as she maneuvered her car on the bridge. Built in the seventies, the two mile long bridge connected the barrier island of Pelican Cove to the mainland.

"Actually, this is very much like me. I'm famous for being low on confidence."

"Not in our world," Heather pointed out. "You're a brave woman, Jenny. One of the strongest I have ever met. I look up to you."

Jenny flashed a grateful look at the young girl sitting beside her. Heather and Molly had come to mean a lot to her. She cherished their new friendship more than the ones she had left behind. None of the women she had hobnobbed with for the past twenty years had cared to ask after her. She had become persona non grata in the suburban soccer mom club as soon as her husband traded her in for a new model. At forty four, Jenny had given up all hopes of finding any new friends again. The Magnolias had helped her believe.

"What do you think of Jason's new girl friend?" Heather asked suddenly.

"Jason has a girl friend?" Jenny asked, swerving to avoid some debris on the road.

"Kandy?" Heather reminded her. "She's so posh."

"I didn't know Jason was going out with her."

Jenny made a left to enter another small town. Heather gave her directions until she pulled up in front of a small Cape Cod tucked away in a cul de sac. Jenny needn't have worried about her reception.

A slim woman with a salt and pepper bob greeted them at the door. Her gray eyes were warm and the smile on her face seemed genuine. She offered them coffee or tea. Jenny added sugar to her coffee and stirred it as she thought of how to begin.

"Try these cookies," the woman said. "They are fresh out of the oven."

"Thank you for seeing me, Mrs. Turner," Jenny began. "I know this might be painful for you."

"Our Emily's been gone twenty six years," the woman sighed. "People around these parts barely remember her."

"So you don't mind talking to us about her?" Heather burst out.

"I'll take any chance to talk about my baby."

"It must be hard on you," Jenny sympathized.

Jenny couldn't bear the thought of losing her son Nick. She couldn't imagine how this woman had survived all these years without any news of her daughter.

"I try to keep her memory alive."

The woman pointed to an array of photographs on the mantel. Jenny guessed they all portrayed the missing girl. There were photos of her at all ages – a bonny baby, a gap toothed toddler, a girl in pig tails, and an older girl looking grownup in a sleeveless frock and a strand of pearls around her neck.

There were several photos of the grownup girl and Jenny peered at them curiously, trying to ignore a feeling of déjà vu. Goosebumps broke out on her body as she realized why the girl looked familiar.

"Are the police still looking for your girl?"

The woman dabbed a tissue at her eyes and shook her head.

"Although she's still listed as missing, they stopped looking for her long ago."

"Did she ever contact you?"

Mrs. Turner shook her head.

"Never. I would give anything to know she's okay. I just want her to be safe and happy wherever she is."

"Did she say why she was leaving?"

"She went out for a party one Saturday evening," Mrs. Turner said hoarsely. "She never came back."

"Did you have any disagreements?" Jenny asked politely. "Any reason she might have run away?"

"My Emily was a good girl. She had a 4.0 GPA. She sang in the church choir. She was all set to go to an Ivy League college."

Emily Turner sounded perfect. Jenny wondered what had made her leave home.

"Was she involved with anyone?"

"She was going out with a local boy," Mrs. Turner told them. "We knew his folks well. He knew Emily since middle school."

"Did she tell him anything?"

"The police questioned him, of course. He didn't know about that party she went to."

"Could she have been seeing someone else?"

"I wouldn't have believed that once," Mrs. Turner said sadly. "But now, who knows? I have come up with plenty of theories over the years. None of them brought my girl back."

"I'm sorry, Mrs. Turner," Jenny apologized again.

"Why are you asking about this now?" the woman asked suddenly.

"I was doing some research on missing women," Jenny said lamely. "It's a project I am working on."

"Who told you about Emily?"

"I came across some old newspaper clippings," Jenny told her honestly.

"All the local newspapers wrote about it," Mrs. Turner nodded. "We even printed a message for her in the papers, begging her to come back home."

"Did Emily ever go to Pelican Cove?" Jenny asked in a hushed voice.

"I don't think so. She didn't have a car. We were going to buy her a new one after her high school graduation."

"But she had friends who drove cars?" Jenny asked. "She went out with them?"

"She must have," Mrs. Turner sighed. "She was always home before curfew so we didn't keep tabs on her. Maybe we should have."

Jenny and Heather said their goodbyes and promised to keep in touch with Mrs. Turner. Jenny couldn't wait to get in her car.

"Something's got you hot and bothered," Heather noted as Jenny peeled out of the driveway. "Spill it."

"Those photos on the mantel ... anything ring a bell?"

"I didn't really look. It was kind of sad. Why?"

"She's the girl in the locket," Jenny burst out. "I'm sure of it."

"You mean the locket you found in that dead guy's room?"

"Your grandma confirmed the boy in the photo was Keith. But she didn't know who the girl was. I am sure it was Emily."

"So Keith knew Emily?"

Jenny's head was buzzing with different scenarios.

"You don't carry just anyone's photo in a locket. Keith not only knew Emily, I'm willing to bet he was in love with her."

"But she had a boyfriend in her own town. You just heard what her mother said."

"Think like a teenager, Heather. You have a steady boyfriend but you meet some boy in another town. Wouldn't you keep him hidden?"

"I never had eyes for anyone other than Chris," Heather said sadly.

"Never mind that," Jenny dismissed. "Think hypothetically."

"Keith was a junkie, remember? Maybe that's why Emily didn't want to tell her parents about him. She wanted to maintain her goody-goody image."

"That makes perfect sense," Jenny crowed, banging her hand on the steering wheel.

"Slow down, Jenny," Heather shrieked. "Do you want a speeding ticket?"

Jenny forced herself to calm down.

"What do they say about the scene of the crime?" she said out loud. "Something about the criminal always going back."

"What are you hinting at?"

"Why did Keith come to Pelican Cove? Why now? Why after all these years?"

"My guess is he wanted to squeeze some money from you. He just wanted to score more drugs, Jenny."

"Or, he read about the skeleton they found at Seaview and couldn't stay away."

Jenny pulled up outside the Bayview Inn and placed an arm on Heather's shoulder.

"What if our Mrs. Bones is actually Miss Bones?"

Heather stared back at Jenny, her eyes growing big as saucers.

"Are you serious, Jenny?"

Jenny had to spell it out.

"What if Mrs. Bones is Emily Turner?"

Chapter 14

Jenny spent a sleepless night mulling over her theory. She wanted to run it by Jason before presenting it to Adam. She was sure Adam wouldn't be receptive to anything she put forth.

Jenny confirmed Jason was in his office before going over. She took over a box of chocolate cupcakes. Jason was a big fan of anything chocolate.

"How's my favorite client this morning?" Jason beamed.

Jason always had a pleasant countenance but his smile seemed a bit brighter than usual to Jenny.

"You look happy."

"I was thinking about last night. Kandy and I had dinner in Virginia Beach. It was magical."

Jenny feared what Heather had told her was true.

"Are you and Kandy a thing now?"

"I don't know, Jenny. Do you think she'll have me?"

"And why shouldn't she?"

"Have you looked at her? She's smart and beautiful.

She has a reputation in court, I can tell you that."

"Any girl will be lucky to have you by her side."

"I wish," Jason murmured cryptically.

He bit into a cupcake and quirked an eyebrow at her.

"So? What's up?"

Jenny told him about her visit to Mrs. Turner.

"What are you getting at, Jenny?"

"What if our Mrs. Bones is Emily Turner?"

"How did she end up here?"

"That's what we have to find out. It's not impossible."

"Let's start with what she was doing in Pelican Cove."

Jenny told him about the locket then.

"Are you sure it's the same girl? How many times did you look at this locket?"

"I'm sure. We can always compare the two photos."

"So you are thinking Keith Bennet knew this girl."

"You don't just carry any random girl's photo in a locket, Jason. Keith knew her very well. I'm willing to bet they had something going."

"Let's say you're right for a moment. Are you saying Keith killed that poor girl? Why on earth would he do that?"

"It could have been an accident," Jenny mused. "She came here to meet him. They quarreled about something. He could have hit her or pushed her or something."

"And then he buried her in his own backyard?"

"Too farfetched?"

"What about his family? You think no one noticed?"

"He had none by that time. His sister was gone and Lily had already run away. His father worked out of town, remember? He might not have been at home all the time."

"Did Keith look like a killer to you?"

"He was a drug addict. He might have done it for money."

Jason stood up and began pacing the floor.

"Say you're right. Why would he carry the girl's photo on a chain all these years? He had to have some feelings for her."

"Who says he didn't?" Jenny argued. "Maybe he spent his life repenting over it."

"So why do you think he came back? When I was working on the Seaview sale, we looked really hard for him. He chose not to turn up at that time."

"All the local papers carried the story about Mrs. Bones," Jenny said. "He must have read it. He wanted to come and look for himself."

"It's not as if they have Mrs. Bones on display."

Jenny shook her head.

"I don't know why he came back. He must have missed her. Maybe he wanted to keep his ear to the ground, see what the police found out about her."

"Did you tell the girl's mother about this?"

"Of course not!" Jenny said indignantly. "I know this is just a theory."

"We still need to talk to the police about it."

"You think Adam will listen to me?"

"You need to tell them about the girl in the photo. I think it's a possible line of investigation. Let the police decide what they want to do with it. You don't want to be accused of hiding relevant information."

They crossed the street and entered the police station two doors down. Nora greeted Jenny with a smile. She pointed at Adam's door.

Adam sat with his leg propped up, immersed in a mountain of files.

"Why do we need paperwork?" he scowled at them.

Jenny and Jason sat down without waiting for an invitation. Adam gave Jenny a warm smile. A secret message passed between them. Jenny knew he wouldn't cut her any slack though.

She began her story. Adam warded her off almost immediately.

"You think this girl, Emily Turner, has been lying in your garden all these years? Isn't that a leap of faith?"

"I tracked down most of the missing women from the region," Jenny explained. "Some came back, some were found dead. There were very few who are still reported missing."

"So there are more than one?"

"What about the locket?" Jenny asked him.

"I think you are mistaken. I'm not eager to go down to these Turners and disturb them."

"I met the woman," Jenny said soberly. "She's hungry for any information about her daughter."

"She could have lied to you," Adam mused. "Maybe they knew the girl was seeing Keith. He was slightly older, right? And he was a junkie. They might not have approved of him."

"So you agree there's some connection?" Jenny asked.

"I don't know, Jenny," Adam sighed. "It's hardly relevant now. Keith is dead."

"Exactly. And we don't know how he died."

Adam cleared his throat.

"Actually, we might. We think he took his own life. It will probably be ruled as accident or suicide."

"Keith didn't seem depressed to me," Jenny objected.

"Doesn't matter what you think," Adam snapped. "The case is almost closed now."

"Does that mean Jenny is not a suspect?" Jason asked.

"Yes. That's good news for you, Jenny. You can let go of this now."

"What about Mrs. Bones? What if she is Emily Turner?"

"We are still waiting on reports."

"There are so many tests you can do now. The Turners need some closure."

"Don't tell me how to do my job, Jenny," Adam said patiently.

"Why is he never receptive to my ideas?" Jenny complained to Jason as they walked out. "You want to come eat lunch with me?"

"Sorry Jenny, I'm meeting Kandy for lunch."

"Hot date, huh?" Jenny kidded.

She couldn't explain the green eyed monster that had suddenly reared its head.

"It's a working lunch," Jason laughed. "I need some help on one of my cases. Turns out it's Kandy's area of expertise."

"That's convenient."

Jason peered at Jenny's face.

"Are you alright, Jenny? You look a bit pale."

"I'm fine," she assured Jason and headed back to the café.

Jenny thought about Keith as a boy living in Pelican

Cove. He must have had some friends. Adam and Jason were both in the same age group but they didn't remember Keith. Jenny was glad to see Captain Charlie sitting at a table in the café.

"Taking a breather," he told her. "I thought I would eat my lunch here today."

Captain Charlie was one of Jenny's regulars. He ate breakfast and lunch at the café everyday but he almost always got his order to go.

Captain Charlie smacked his lips as he sprinkled some Old Bay seasoning on his sandwich.

"Can I ask you something, Captain Charlie?" Jenny asked, sitting down in front of him. "Do you remember Keith Bennet? He lived at Seaview with his family."

"Lily's son?" Captain Charlie asked. "He didn't live here more than a year. Went off to college the year after Lily moved here."

"Did he have any friends? Who did he hang out with?"

"Was a loner," Captain Charlie said, scratching his head. "Roamed around on the bluffs by himself. Took pity on him and offered him a job but he said no."

"He was a lazy bum then?"

"You could say that," Captain Charlie nodded. "That's why I was surprised when he got himself a girl."

Jenny's ears pricked up. "Girl?"

"Pretty chit too, although I'm willing to bet she was a lot younger than him. Wasn't from around here."

"Did you know her name?" Jenny asked eagerly.

Captain Charlie shook his head.

"Saw them in the dark a few times, taking a boat out or sitting on that beach in front of your house."

"Would you recognize her if I showed you a photo?"

"It was a long time ago. My memory's not what it used to be."

"Aren't you hungry yet, Jenny?" Petunia called from the kitchen. "Time to close up."

Jenny munched on chicken salad as she went over all the facts again.

"What are you frowning about?" Petunia asked.

"Nothing. Did we use up all the salad?"

Jenny trudged to the seafood market on her way home. Chris was checking out packages at a counter, dressed in a formal shirt and trousers.

"Going somewhere?"

"I had an open house this morning. It went well."

Chris seemed eager to talk to her.

"I've let my realtor business slide. I'm going to ramp it up again. Molly won't have to worry about her job if I make good money."

Jenny wondered if Chris was putting the cart before the horse but she stayed quiet.

"Money always helps," she said lamely.

"What can I get you, Jenny?" Chris asked.

Jenny asked for her usual order, a pound of shelled and deveined shrimp and rockfish steaks. She ordered three guessing Jimmy Parsons would be joining them for dinner.

"Did you talk to Heather?" Chris asked. "How is she taking this?"

"She will be fine, Chris," Jenny said diplomatically.

"I still care for her, you know," Chris said. "I want her to be happy."

"Give it time," Jenny advised. "Things will sort themselves out."

Star and Jimmy Parsons were sitting out on the patio overlooking the garden.

"Are you ready to move in permanently?" Jenny asked her aunt.

"Let's wait for a while," Star said. "I'll feel better once they get to the bottom of this mystery."

She tipped her head at the garden and Jenny understood what she was referring to. Once again, Jenny told her what she had found out.

"So that boy you met killed this young girl. But who killed him?"

"I've thought about it dozens of times. My head's pounding right now."

"You ladies need to do something fun for a change," Jimmy spoke up. "How about some board games?"

"There's just the three of us," Jenny complained.

"We can fix that," Star smiled broadly.

She went in and placed a few calls. A couple of cars drew up outside. Molly and Chris came in followed by Adam. Tank bounded in on his heels.

Jenny greeted the dog with open arms.

"Tank! You're just the tonic I needed."

Tank showed his appreciation by licking her face down.

"I took care of dinner," Adam told her. "You just relax and put your feet up. No more sleuthing tonight."

"You're not mad at me?" Jenny murmured.

"You can be a pain, Jenny," Adam said, taking his hands in hers. "But there's always some logic in what you say."

"Does that mean …"

"What did I tell you?" Adam raised his eyebrows. "You're just going to drink some wine, eat junk food and have a good time with your friends."

"Keith didn't have any friends. Captain Charlie told me he was a loner."

"You talked to Captain Charlie about Keith Bennet?" Adam shook his head in wonder. "You're a dynamo, Jenny."

The bell rang and a delivery guy from Mama Rosa's brought in big boxes of pizza and salad.

"Olives and artichokes!" Jenny exclaimed. "That's my favorite."

She looked up into Adam's eyes and smiled adoringly.

"You remembered."

"Of course I did," he said, chucking her under the chin.

Jenny took a sip of her wine and settled against Adam on her new couch. He placed his arm around her.

Seaview rang with the laughter of friends. The roses and gardenias bloomed in the garden and for a few hours, everyone forgot about the gruesome events that had taken place at that house.

Chapter 15

The Magnolias sat sipping their morning coffee on the deck of the Boardwalk Café, sampling the pumpkin bread Jenny had baked that day.

"Not too sweet," Betty Sue remarked, licking her lips. "I like that."

"It's got a kick," Molly said. "It's a bit different from the pumpkin spice I'm used to."

"I'm trying out a special blend," Jenny told them. "I'm thinking of selling this pumpkin bread during the read-a-thon."

"That glaze makes it super yum," Heather said, wiping some crumbs from her mouth.

"So are we all going to volunteer to read for this event?" Star asked. "I'm not sure what we are supposed to do exactly."

"It's not complicated," Jenny stressed. "Just go sit there, pick up your favorite book and read."

"What if Betty Sue and I want to read the same book?"

"Two people can read the same book, but you can't read the same book twice."

Star made a face.

"Don't make it more difficult."

"I'm not," Jenny laughed. "You'll catch on when the time comes. I'm hoping to put in at least a couple of hours every day. I would do more but I have to take care of the concession stand too."

"I'm reading as much as they allow me to," Molly declared.

"Me too," Betty Sue nodded. "I used to read a lot when I was a child."

Betty Sue's face changed as she thought about old times.

"Lily and I both read a lot. We swapped books all the time."

"Any news about Keith?" Heather asked Jenny.

"The police are saying he took his own life," Jenny said stonily.

"And you don't agree, I guess?" Heather quipped. "Why not?"

"It's just a hunch."

"You were wondering why he came here," Molly

mused. "Maybe it was sort of like a last wish. He wanted to see his old town and his old home, a place where he must have been happy."

"That makes sense," Star agreed. "Poor guy."

"I say he wasn't in his senses," Betty Sue said hoarsely. "He was lost in some drug induced stupor. He didn't realize what he was doing."

Jason called Jenny at the café that afternoon. He had never done that before.

"Are you winding up over there?"

"I'll be done in about thirty minutes. Why?"

"Come to my office. I have some news."

Jenny rushed through her chores and walked down the street to Jason's office, taking some of her pumpkin bread for him.

She couldn't wait to learn why he had summoned her so urgently.

"Quick, tell me what's wrong."

"Nothing's wrong," Jason said. "Just some new developments."

Jenny put her hands on her hips and raised her

eyebrows.

"What are you waiting for?"

"Ann Davis is in town with her son."

"Ann Davis as in the woman I bought my house from?"

"That's the one."

"Why are they here?"

"They are here for Keith. Other than his father who is in a home, they are his only surviving family."

"Okay!" Jenny quipped. "So where's the fire?"

"Why don't you sit down?" Jason motioned to a chair in front of his desk.

Jenny flopped down and clasped her hands together.

"They are not very happy about the suicide theory. They are at the police station, talking to Adam right now."

"What do they say then?"

"They believe he was killed, Jenny."

"And what do they want?"

"I believe they want justice for Keith."

"Where were they when he was roaming around the country doing drugs?"

"We don't know anything about that," Jason sighed.

"You told me yourself. You couldn't get in touch with Keith."

"I'm beginning to wonder if I didn't look hard enough," Jason said sheepishly.

"What do you mean?"

"All those ads in the paper, those attempts to contact Keith ... Ricky Davis took charge of all that. Maybe he lied to me."

"We never discussed the legalities behind the Seaview deal," Jenny said. "Was Keith listed as an owner?"

"Old man Davis listed all his grandkids as owners. Rick and Keith were the only living grandchildren. Although Ann was listed as the owner after her husband died, the grandchildren had equal rights to the house."

"So you needed Keith and Ricky to sign off on the house deal. How did you do that without Keith?"

"Ricky has a power of attorney," Jason explained. "We tried hard to contact Keith but I always knew there was a way out if he didn't turn up."

"Doesn't sound like they were close though," Jenny muttered. "Why has Ann made this trip?"

"You can ask her yourself. They want to meet you."

"Why?"

"I guess we'll know soon enough," Jason said as he spotted someone out on the street.

There was a knock on the office door and an old lady tottered in, leaning on a man's arm. Her snow white hair and craggy face hinted at an advanced age. She looked so frail Jenny thought the slightest puff of wind would blow her away. The widow's peak on her forehead split it into two equal parts.

Ricky Davis was tall and hefty with bluish gray eyes that bore into hers. He settled his mother into a chair and leaned against a wall himself.

Jason made the introductions.

"You look young," Ann Davis noted. "When I heard someone was interested in that old pile of dust, I pictured someone older."

Jenny said nothing.

"You wanted to talk to me?"

"You seem to have quite a reputation in town," Ricky cut to the chase. "How about using your skills to find what happened to Keith?"

Jenny protested.

"I'm not a professional investigator. I have a lot on my plate right now."

"Jason says you met him?" Ricky pressed. "Did he look like someone who was planning to take his life?"

Jenny thought for a minute.

"I talked to him a couple of times. Honestly, I can't tell what his state of mind was. It's not like I knew him. I had never met him before."

"Did he say why he was here?"

"Not in so many words," Jenny said. "Clearly, he wasn't happy that Seaview had been sold."

She looked pointedly at Ricky.

"It seems you didn't exactly take his permission before selling me the house?"

"Keith never cared for the house all these years," Ricky said forcefully. "You think we haven't wanted to come here? I suggested we clean up the place, spend the summer here. But Keith always wanted to stay away."

"I guess he doesn't have good memories about the place."

"You don't know the half of it," Ricky said.

"Poor Keith," Ann finally spoke. "He had a troubled life."

"Did you know he was a junkie?"

"I don't like that word," Ann said softly. "Keith lost his way."

"He was an ex-addict," Ricky told them. "Keith had been sober for three years. That's why I can't believe he died of an overdose."

"The police are saying he injected himself."

"He was very serious about his sobriety," Ann said. "We sent him to a recovery center a few years ago. He did very well in the program. He turned over a new leaf after that."

"Couldn't he have had a relapse? Coming here might have rekindled the past."

"That's what you can find out for us," Ricky pleaded.

"May I ask why you are doing this?" Jenny asked. "I thought you were estranged."

"He was a bit of a drifter," Ricky admitted. "He moved from town to town whenever it pleased him. He didn't always keep in touch with us. But he was the only family I had."

"The boys were very close growing up," Ann said, dabbing her eyes with her tissue. "You know I lost one child in the storm? Keith was like my second son. Lily should have never come back here."

"We drifted apart after Keith moved here," Ricky nodded. "I spent a lot of years trying to reconnect with him like old times."

"We lost the real Keith a long time ago," Ann agreed.

"I just want to find out what happened to my brother," Ricky said emphatically. "Can you understand that?"

"I'll see what I can do," Jenny said reluctantly. "But I can't make any promises."

"We are staying at the Bayview Inn while we are in town," Ricky told her. "You can reach us there if you want to."

Ann Davis was looking exhausted.

"We have been traveling since last night," Ricky said. "It has taken a toll on my mother."

"Betty Sue and Heather will take good care of you,"

Jenny smiled. "We can meet again tomorrow."

Jason and Jenny both stood up as Ricky helped his mother to her feet.

"Why don't you come to Seaview for dinner?" Jenny said suddenly. "It's like a new place altogether."

Ann's face clouded over.

"I'm not sure I want to set foot in that house again," she said weakly. "Look what happened to Keith."

Jenny was speechless. She pasted a fake smile on her face while Jason ushered the Davises out.

"Do people realize I actually live there?" Jenny cried. "Why do people keep on bad mouthing my home?"

"Just ignore them."

Jason sat down and spotted the box Jenny had brought over. He took a big bite of the pumpkin bread and groaned in pleasure.

"Does this come in chocolate?"

"It's pumpkin bread, you fool," Jenny laughed. "I'll put some chocolate chips in it for you next time."

"So?" Jason asked. "What do you think of them?"

"I'm still not sure why they are here."

"I have no doubt you'll find out soon enough."

"Have you volunteered for the read-a-thon yet?"

"Kandy and I both have," Jason said eagerly. "She's invited some of her lawyer friends. They have deep pockets, Jenny, very deep pockets."

"So you told Kandy about the issues at the library?"

"There's something about her, Jenny," Jason said, his eyes full of passion. "We talk about every topic on earth. I never thought I could get along so well with anyone."

"That's good of her."

"She loves libraries," Jason said, bobbing his head. "She grew up poor and the library was the only place she could hang out at and study. She worked at a library for many years until she became a lawyer."

Jenny wondered what else the virtuous Kandy could lay claim to.

"She sounds perfect for you."

"I'm not sure if she sees me that way," Jason confessed.

"How many dates have you been on?"

"More than a few," Jason agreed.

"You need to be bolder, Jason," Jenny said lightly. "Take the plunge."

Jason had a laid back personality. He didn't believe in pressuring anyone.

"Is that where I went wrong, Jenny?" Jason asked suddenly. "I know I'm not as aggressive as Adam."

"I love you just the way you are," Jenny said, and almost bit her lip. "You know what I mean."

Jason's expression was inscrutable.

"I'm happy for you, Jason. I'll be looking out for Kandy during the read-a-thon."

"She won't miss talking to you," Jason said. "She's sponsoring a prize. Dinner for two at a big city restaurant for the first person to finish reading all Jane Austen books."

"That's a great idea! Maybe we can give out a few prizes for meals at the café. I am going to talk to Petunia about it."

Jenny pushed back her chair and stifled a yawn.

"What's going to be your first step?" Jason asked.

"I need to get some more background on Keith. I am going to talk to Ann again tomorrow."

"Any more updates from Adam?"

"Why don't you ask him, Jason? You have a better chance of getting a civil response out of him."

"So we are ruling out suicide?"

"We are. At least until I eliminate all other possible scenarios."

Chapter 16

Molly was smiling to herself as she drank her coffee.

"What are you thinking about, girl?" Star asked.

"Chris took me out in a canoe last night," Molly gushed. "It was so romantic."

"You actually convinced him to take time out from stacking shelves?" Heather sniffed. "Good for you."

Molly said nothing, wrapped up as she was in pleasant thoughts.

"Ann Davis looks old," Betty Sue remarked, setting her knitting down. "Have you seen those wrinkles on her face?"

The other women tried not to smile. Betty Sue could be vain about her looks. Jenny had to admit she was quite well preserved for someone in her eighties.

"Did she remember you?" she asked.

"Lily and I were joined at the hip. I was in and out of that house all the time. Of course she remembered me."

"Did she mention Lily?" Star asked softly.

Betty Sue's face fell.

"Not yet. What's there to talk about but old memories?"

"Did Lily ever contact her in all these years?"

"You think Ann would mention it if she had?" Betty Sue's face looked hopeful.

"What are they doing here now?" Star asked. "Mother and son?"

"They were going to walk around in town. That shouldn't take too long."

"Did Ann ever visit after Lily came back?" Jenny asked.

"I don't know. You'll have to ask her that."

"So she's been gone since 1962. That's over fifty five years."

Betty Sue stared at the ocean moodily. Jenny guessed the Davis family was going to stir up a lot of painful memories for her friend.

Heather had barely looked up from her phone all this time. She suddenly looked up with a shout.

"I have a date!"

"It's time you stopped meeting these strangers," Betty Sue said curtly. "It's not safe."

"It's not a stranger, Grandma. It's Duster."

"That guy you met in the summer?" Jenny remembered. "What's he doing here this time of the year."

Duster and his family had rented a house up the coast for the summer.

"He has a new sales job," Heather read off the screen. "He's on a tour of the area and wants to catch up."

She looked at Molly.

"His cousin's been asking about you."

"You can tell him I'm seeing someone," Molly grinned broadly.

"We all know that, Molly," Heather snapped. "No need to rub it in."

The lunch rush kept Jenny off her feet. A familiar couple walked up the steps around 1 PM. The café was almost empty.

"Are you serving lunch?" Ricky Davis asked cheerfully. "We thought we would check here before driving out of town."

"Of course," Jenny said with a smile. "Pick any table you want."

"How about out on the deck?"

"Be my guest," Jenny said, looking at Ann Davis. "It's a bit windy though."

"I'll keep my coat on. I can't get enough of the ocean."

"Do you live near the coast?" she asked politely, trying to make conversation.

"We live in the driest part of Texas," Ann grumbled. "No beaches around us for sure. That's the one thing I miss most about this place."

Jenny told them about the day's specials.

"I have mushroom and wild rice soup, autumn chicken salad or oyster po'boys. I can also rustle up a crab salad if you want."

Ricky and Ann told her what they wanted.

"Did you grow up around these parts?" Jenny asked curiously.

"My family came to this part of the world two hundred years ago," Ann nodded. "We lived in a town up north on the Maryland border. I met my Roy at a country dance. It was love at first sight for us."

"So you still have family in these parts?"

"There's an old aunt," Ann noted. "Most of the others have moved away for jobs."

Jenny went inside and started assembling their lunch. Petunia fried a basket full of oysters and handed them over to Jenny. Jenny took the soup out and set it before mother and son.

Ricky Davis looked relaxed, stretched out in his chair with his arms around his head.

"My mom never said how beautiful this place was," he sighed.

"Is this the first time you are visiting Pelican Cove?" Jenny asked.

"I came to visit Aunt Lily, but not since the family moved out."

Jenny slathered her special tartar sauce on fresh rolls from the local bakery. She piled a generous helping of fried oysters onto each roll. Ann Davis reached for the canister of Old Bay seasoning before biting into her sandwich.

"Care to join us?" Ricky asked.

"I can sit with you," Jenny agreed, pulling out a chair.

"What's going on with the library?" Ann asked. "Surely it's not closing down?"

"Not yet, I hope," Jenny smiled. "We are doing everything we can to prevent that from happening."

"My husband's grandfather was one of the founders of the Pelican Cove Library," Ann told her. "He laid the foundation stone. It's part of the family legacy, in a way."

"We are having a read-a-thon to raise funds," Jenny supplied. "Why don't you participate?"

"You can count on our support," Ann told her. She looked at her son. "Write a check for them, Ricky."

"Can I ask you something about Keith?" Jenny ventured. "It's sort of delicate."

"The boy's already gone," Ann said bitterly. "No use tiptoeing around."

Jenny clasped her hands and struggled to find the right words.

"We found an old chain in Keith's room. It was a bit tarnished. I don't think it was valuable."

"Did it have a locket?" Ricky asked.

"Yes."

"Keith's been wearing that chain since he was nineteen. He never took it off."

"About that locket …" Jenny hesitated. "There was a picture in it. Actually there were two photos. Betty Sue confirmed one of them was Keith. The other was a girl."

Ann's neck jerked up as she stared at her son.

"A young girl?" she asked softly.

"Emily," Ricky said under his breath.

"So you can confirm that was Emily Turner?" Jenny asked sharply.

"How do you know that?" Ricky asked incredulously.

"It's a long story," Jenny sighed. "Let's say I saw her photo somewhere else and it rang a bell."

"I wish Keith had never met that girl," Ann cried.

"Was she his girl friend?"

Ricky shook his head as he chewed on his sandwich.

"Keith was madly in love with her. And we thought she loved him too, until she left him."

"Left him?" Jenny questioned. "Why do you say that?"

"She was younger than him, you know," Ricky told her. "Still a junior in high school. She hitched rides to come to Pelican Cove to meet Keith."

"Wasn't that dangerous?"

"Keith told her that. He used to meet her as often as he could. They talked about eloping."

"What did her parents feel about that?"

"She hadn't told them about Keith. She had a boyfriend back home, a kid her age."

"What happened?"

"Emily didn't turn up one day," Ricky explained. "It was the summer of 1991. I was here in town. My uncle had decided to close the house and move to a place near us. Keith didn't want to leave without Emily."

"Emily is still missing," Jenny said grimly. "She left for a party one night and never went back home."

"Keith thought she ran away with someone else."

"Why would he think that?" Jenny asked. "Didn't he trust her at all?"

"It had been a hard year for Keith," Ann explained. "His sister died a few months ago. Lily ran away that spring. He was grieving over them. Meeting this girl changed him."

"It was almost as if he was ready to live again," Ricky nodded. "Everything came crashing down when Emily left."

"Why do you keep saying that?" Jenny demanded. "How do you know she left voluntarily? She could have been attacked or had an accident."

"Keith always believed she ditched him," Ricky said sadly. "Like his mother."

"Lily did a number on her family when she abandoned them," Ann quavered. "Keith was never the same again."

"It was the beginning of his downfall," Ricky agreed.

"He was in college then, wasn't he?"

"He was a freshman," Ricky nodded. "But he never went back."

"He was smart," Ann shrugged. "But he never made use of his mind. He started doing drugs. He almost died a couple of times."

"What about his father?"

"Lily's husband boarded up the house and moved to Texas. Keith came with him. His father tried to reason with him for years. Keith never held a job or met anyone else. He used to disappear for months. Then he turned up when he wanted money."

Jenny could hear the regret in Ricky's voice.

"Do you believe Emily ran away?" Jenny asked Ricky.

"I don't know," he shrugged. "I didn't know her well. Sometimes I think that's why Keith roamed around like a vagabond. He was hoping to run into her somewhere."

"What about this latest rehab Jason mentioned?"

"Three years ago, Keith came to us," Ann began. "He wanted to start over. He wanted to take a stab at living a normal life. He sounded committed. Of course we wanted the same thing for him. We put him in the finest recovery clinic in the state. He got through the program and got a job."

"He was doing fine," Ricky muttered. "Then he fell off the radar again. We had no idea he had come to Pelican Cove."

Jenny's heart was heavy. She offered to serve dessert. Ricky and Ann both declined.

"We ate your muffins for breakfast," Ann remarked. "They were delicious."

"Where are you headed now?"

"I want to see the light house," Ann said. "We used to climb up to the top, Roy and I. My Ricky was conceived there on our third anniversary."

"Mother!" Ricky Davis groaned.

"Jimmy Parsons will show you around."

"Those Parsons are still around then?" Ann looked at her son. "One of those kids used to take you up there to show you the light."

"Did Keith have any enemies?" Jenny asked suddenly.

"He was aloof. He barely talked to anyone. I don't think he knew anyone well enough to make friends or enemies."

"What about those men he bought drugs from?" Ann asked suddenly.

"That's right," Jenny said. "Drug dealers are an unsavory lot."

"Keith was pretty good about paying up. His father did very well and set up a trust fund for him. Cash was never his problem."

"He must have met someone in all these years?" Jenny persisted. "What about that rehab you sent him to?

Did he make any friends there?"

"Not that I know of." Ricky shook his head.

"What about women?" Jenny mused. "Was he seeing anyone?"

"Emily was the only girl for him."

"What if he fell for someone though? Maybe he wanted to get a fresh start in life. He could have come here to say farewell. Say goodbye to the last place he met Emily."

Jenny wondered if she sounded crazy. Truth be told, she was grasping at straws.

"I wondered if there was a woman," Rick admitted. "Especially when he wanted to clean up three years ago. I didn't know what else would motivate him that much. But he never introduced us to anyone."

"Lily's family came to a sad end," Ann said grimly. "She should have never come back here."

A hundred thoughts clamored in Jenny's head as she walked home. She had come to Pelican Cove later in life, just like Lily. She had dragged her son along with her too. Jenny couldn't help but notice the similarities between her life and Lily's. Granted, Lily's husband hadn't dumped her. But they must have had their differences. Why else had Lily left her happy family behind to run away with another man? Had losing her daughter driven her off the edge? Keith had suffered a similar fate. Maybe insanity ran in the Davis family.

Chapter 17

Jenny tapped her head with a pencil, going over the menu once again. She had been discussing what they would sell at the concession stand with Petunia.

"Normally I would just do coffee and muffins," Petunia told her. "But you have made a name for yourself. I already have requests from people."

"Heather says there have been some comments on Instagram too," Jenny said shyly. "People want to taste our seafood. And they are asking for everything from soup to sandwiches to pies."

"We need to keep the menu simple," Petunia spoke from experience. "It has to be something we can make in big quantities without too much effort."

"It's getting chilly," Jenny remarked. "We definitely need soup."

"Choose any three soups – one a day." Petunia had planned menus for many events. "Pumpkin soup, chicken soup and seafood chowder."

"We can have one sandwich for every day too," Jenny said, catching on. "chicken salad, egg salad and tomato cheese."

"Now you just have to choose the desserts," Petunia smiled. "We need cookies, lots and lots of cookies."

"Have you thought of the prizes the Boardwalk Café will sponsor?"

"Lunch for two," Petunia said, "and your special chocolate cake. We can give away a couple of both of these. That's as much as we can afford."

"Whatever you say, Petunia," Jenny agreed.

Jenny knew these prizes were small fry compared to what some other people were offering. But they just wanted to pitch in and do their bit. She thought of the money Ann Davis had promised to donate. Did Ann have a private income or was her son Ricky going to shell out the money. Jenny realized she didn't know much about them at all.

"What do we know about them, really?" Jenny asked Adam as they were walking on the beach later that night.

"You don't like them, I take it?"

"It's not a question of liking or not liking anyone. We have to think about people connected to Keith. He wasn't married so there is no spouse to worry about. His father's an invalid. Ann and Ricky are his only family."

"And you suspect them of wrongdoing?" Adam asked with a smile. "You are beginning to think like a detective, Jenny."

"If that's a compliment, I will take it."

Tank walked beside them, wagging his tail. Jenny lapsed into silence, focusing on throwing a stick for Tank to fetch.

"Have you made any progress regarding Keith?" she finally asked Adam.

"I can't talk about that," Adam protested.

"So you still think it's suicide? I can't believe that."

"Why not? You know he had a history of drug abuse. He was mooning over some girl. The man was unstable, Jenny."

"What about Mrs. Bones? Any update on her?"

"She's low on the list of priorities. All I know is they are running tests."

"You don't think Keith killed Emily Turner and buried her in his backyard?"

Adam burst out laughing. Jenny turned red and glared at him but Adam couldn't stop.

"I already told you that's farfetched, Jenny."

"But why? We know Emily left home to go to some party out of town. She might have been meeting Keith."

"Why did Keith kill her?"

"They had a lover's spat. Things got out of hand. Keith hit her or maybe she fell. He might have panicked."

Adam shook his head in denial. Jenny found herself getting incensed.

"No one found a single trace of Emily. And she never got in touch with her family again. I'm willing to bet she's gone, Adam."

"You think Keith came here to look at the grave?"

"He must have read about the skeleton somewhere. He came here to see what was going on."

"If he had really buried her there, he would have run to the other end of the country."

"He felt some kind of compulsion. Isn't that how it's supposed to be?"

"So he was a crazy, psycho boyfriend who was drawn here by a bag of bones? You can believe that but you don't believe he took his own life?"

Jenny had no answer for that.

Adam walked her back to Seaview and bid her goodnight. Star was watching TV with Jimmy.

"How's the grouch today?" she asked.

"He's not that bad," Jenny protested.

"I still think you should pick Jason," Star griped. She had always been clear about who she thought Jenny should date.

"Jason's found himself a hot girlfriend."

"And whose fault is that?" her aunt called out after her.

Ricky Davis came to the café the next morning. He rubbed his eyes and yawned as Jenny poured him a fresh cup of coffee.

"They ran out of muffins at the inn. That's what I get for sleeping in."

"How's your mother?"

"She's staying in bed this morning. She's not used to all this activity, poor thing."

Jenny wrapped up a couple of muffins for Ricky.

"So what are you going to do today?"

"I'm taking a boat tour to some of the islands," Ricky told her.

"Those are popular with the tourists," Jenny agreed.

"Why are they still sticking around here?" she asked Jason later.

Jason sat in his office with his shirt sleeves rolled up and his tie loose, buried in a mound of paperwork.

"I don't know, Jenny. Maybe they are taking a vacation."

"So they are not really grieving for Keith."

"What are you getting at?"

"What do you know about their background? What does Ricky do for a living, for instance?"

"Ann Davis went back to school after she left town. Her mother took care of Ricky while Ann got her nursing degree. She worked as a nurse for several years. I think she was a private nurse for some rich guy toward the end of her career."

"What about Ricky?"

"He has a good job, enough to have a house and

support a wife and kids. You'll have to ask him more about it."

Jason narrowed his eyes as he looked at Jenny.

"Why this sudden interest? What are you thinking?"

"Where have they been the past couple of weeks? Has anyone asked about their alibi?"

Jason's eyebrows shot up.

"You think they had a hand in Keith's death? You are going too far this time."

"Anything is possible," Jenny insisted. "We don't really know them."

"What possible motive could they have for harming Keith?"

"Ann said Keith's father did well for himself. He had a trust fund. Where does all that money go now?"

"The Davises aren't hurting for money as far as I know."

"Some people can never have enough. Then there's the Seaview sale. They must have pocketed all that money. Then Keith turns up. What if Keith wanted his share?"

"Legally, half of that money did belong to Keith."

Jenny went home and placed a call to the Bayview Inn. She invited Ann Davis and Ricky for dinner. Jason had given her a fancy new grill as a housewarming present. She decided to try it out that night.

Jenny thought about how she would question mother and son. Could she dare to be direct with them? She prepared a dry rub of herbs and spices and rubbed it into chicken thighs. Potatoes boiled in a big stock pot for her warm potato salad. She started chopping vegetables. It was going to be an interesting evening.

Ann Davis looked well rested as she leaned on Ricky's arm. Star and Jimmy greeted them. Jenny had urged Jason to come over. Drinks were poured and appetizers were served.

"This crab dip is delicious," Ricky complimented.

"They don't make crabs like this in Texas," Ann said, scooping some up with a cracker.

"How are you enjoying Pelican Cove?" Star asked. "Jenny told me you took a boat out."

"My Roy used to love going out to the islands," Ann said, reminiscing. "Our family owned some of them, you know. We lost them in the big storm."

"How can you lose an island?" Jenny asked naively.

"They were submerged forever," Jason explained. "Just

like a large part of Morse Isle. Pelican Cove might have been three times what it is now."

"Are you enjoying your time off work?" Jenny asked Ricky.

"It's been a while since I traveled anywhere with Mom. We are having a grand time."

"And you haven't come to Pelican Cove since the 1990s?"

"Not since 1991," Ricky corrected her.

"So you weren't in the area when Keith died?"

Jason stifled a cough and cleared his throat. Ann Davis looked bewildered.

"What are you trying to say, dear?"

"She wants to know where we were when Keith died, Mother," Ricky Davis said, catching on.

His gaze had hardened as he looked at Jenny.

"It's common to ask for alibis of people connected to the victim."

"And you think we were responsible for Keith's death?" Ricky folded his arms and stared at her.

"You asked me to do a job," Jenny argued. "I can't do

it well unless I consider all aspects."

"Did you invite us here to insult us, missy?" Ann croaked. "It's this house. Nothing good ever comes from it."

She struggled to her feet. Ricky sprang into action, helping his mother.

"Would you like a tour?" Jenny asked solicitously. "The contractors did a really fine job. You won't even recognize the place."

Ann ignored her and ordered her son. "Get me out of here."

Ricky started ushering his mother out of the house.

"Please stay!" Jenny urged. "Dinner is almost ready."

"You think I am going to stay here one more minute?" Ann Davis asked sharply.

"Look, I'm sorry, okay. But I had to ask."

"Jenny believes in being thorough," Jason quipped.

"Don't pay attention to my niece," Star said. "She tends to get carried away."

Ann Davis finally calmed down and sat back in her chair.

"I have two weeks off from work," Ricky said. "My wife and I are going through a trial separation. Mom always wanted to visit Pelican Cove. We decided to come here for Keith."

"When did you plan that?"

Ricky looked at Jason.

"We learned Keith had turned up here. I started making travel arrangements. We were coming here anyway. Then Keith died on us."

"So you weren't in Texas when Keith died?"

Ricky put an arm around his mother.

"We were in Northern Virginia, visiting a cousin."

Jenny did the math in her head. Ricky could easily have driven to Pelican Cove and back in a few hours. In fact, he could have come into town at night after his mother went to sleep and got back before she woke up.

She put on her best poker face and smiled.

"That seems like a different country, doesn't it?"

"You don't know how lucky you are," Ann Davis said, extending an olive branch. "We had to use a boat to get to the shore."

"I came to town after they built the bridge," Star said, embarking on one of her favorite stories. "But I never went back. I fell in love and stayed on. Pelican Cove has been my home ever since."

"Funny, isn't it?" Ann mused. "I came here to live with my husband too. But it didn't last long."

Jenny announced dinner was ready. They made small talk as they ate, and the food disappeared quickly. Jenny brought out a lemon cake and cut generous slices. Ricky grabbed her hand when she served him.

"You don't really think I hurt Keith?"

"I need to look for suspects," Jenny said. "I'm just eliminating the possibilities."

"Why would we ask you to look into this if we were guilty? You don't think we are that foolish?"

"I need to find out more about the last month or two of Keith's life. If you know anything about it, please don't keep it from me. The tiniest detail can help."

Ricky blinked as he took a bite of his cake. Jenny was sure she had struck a chord. Ricky was hiding something.

Chapter 18

"People are offering all kinds of prizes," Petunia told the women as they sipped coffee.

Jenny had made pumpkin spice lattes. Heather told her they were a seasonal favorite. Jenny wanted to start offering them at the café and at the concession stand.

"This is a bit spicy for me," Betty Sue said, tasting her coffee.

"I made the spice mix myself," Jenny said proudly. "I can use a bit less the next time."

"What kind of prizes are we talking about?" Star asked.

"The seafood market has offered two dozen oysters to the first person to read a 100 pages."

"That's great," Jenny said, clapping her hands. "That should encourage people to come in early."

"Dinner for two at Ethan's for the person reading the most number of pages in the day," Molly added. "I bet I am going to win that one."

"How many prizes are you angling for, Molly?" Heather said.

Her mouth had twisted in a grimace. It happened every time she spoke to Molly.

"Free pint at the Rusty Anchor for a whole week," Petunia said, reading from a list. "That's going to be popular."

"Barb Norton must be happy," Jenny observed. "The read-a-thon is set to be a major success."

"Have you heard what Ada Newbury promised?" Betty Sue asked. "She's going to match whatever amount we manage to collect."

A collective gasp went up through the group.

Ada Newbury was the richest woman in town. The Newburys had become rich overnight during the big storm of 1962. Rumor had it they had found gold on a nearby shipwreck. Ada liked to flaunt her wealth and was as snooty as they came.

Jenny gave credit where it was due.

"That's very generous of her."

"Showing off," Betty Sue muttered. "Someone mentioned there are going to be TV crews here to cover the event. Ada just wants to get on TV."

"Whatever her reasons, we need the money," Molly said simply. "I'm going to read like I have never read before. That's all I can do."

"The whole town is pitching in and doing something," Petunia reminded her. "We are going to make sure you keep working at that library."

Jenny crossed her fingers and hoped the café would do brisk business at the read-a-thon. They were donating half their profits to the library.

"Any updates on that incident at your house?" Betty Sue asked her, twirling red yarn around her needles.

"The police aren't giving it much importance. Maybe they think it was a stray who wandered up to Seaview."

"He didn't bury himself though, did he?" Betty Sue questioned. "That Hopkins boy needs a kick in his pants."

"I don't think Adam has control over which cases to work on," Jenny argued, coming to his defense.

The Magnolias spent several minutes rehashing the whole incident.

"How are you sleeping these days?" Heather teased. "No weird sounds in the attic? No strange lights?"

"Nothing of that sort," Jenny said good-naturedly. "I sleep like a baby."

"So do I," Star butted in. "Stop harassing my niece, Heather."

Jenny mixed crab salad for lunch and fried a fresh batch of donuts using a new recipe. She wanted to try out a pumpkin spice glaze.

"Woman out there is asking for you," Petunia said, dumping a stack of empty plates in the sink.

"Who is it?"

"Never seen her before." Petunia shrugged. "Doesn't look like a tourist though."

Jenny wiped her hands on a towel and went out. She was surprised to see the woman sitting at a corner table. Crumbling a paper napkin in her hands, she was clearly nervous about being there.

"Mrs. Turner!" Jenny exclaimed. "What brings you here?"

The woman breathed a sigh of relief.

"I thought I would find you here but I wasn't sure."

"I'll get some coffee for us," Jenny said, "or do you prefer lemonade?"

"Coffee's fine," the older woman assured her.

Jenny came out with a tray loaded with coffee and snacks.

"I just ate," Mrs. Turner said.

"These donuts are very popular this season. You have to try them."

The woman seemed to settle down after she took a few bites and sipped her coffee. Jenny let her take her time.

"I've been thinking," Mrs. Turner finally spoke up. "Maybe we should try looking for Emily again."

"That's a great idea," Jenny said, encouraging her. "What did you have in mind?"

"I talked to my husband," the woman said. "It seems you have a reputation."

Jenny dreaded what the woman was going to say next. If the Turners asked her to look for their daughter, would she have to tell them her suspicions? Despite what Adam or Jason had said, Jenny strongly believed that Mrs. Bones was in fact Emily Turner. How could she pretend to look for Emily when her instincts told her she was lying in a police lab somewhere.

"We want you to help us find our daughter."

"Mrs. Turner ..." Jenny hesitated.

"We know what the odds are." The woman rushed ahead. "We have braced ourselves for any outcome. We just want to know."

"I get that, but …"

"Please," the woman urged, tearing up. "What if it were your son or daughter? Wouldn't you want to know?"

"I would," Jenny agreed softly. "I don't know what you heard, Mrs. Turner, but I am not a trained investigator. I just talk to people."

"Just do your best. That will be enough for us."

"We might need to interface with the police," Jenny said tentatively. "Do you have a problem with that?"

"You can do whatever you think needs to be done. We have nothing to hide. If you can get the police to look into such an old case, that will be a coup."

"Technology has changed a lot in the past twenty five years," Jenny said thoughtfully. "We might have more options. I am going to think about this."

"Let us know if you need anything from us."

Jenny asked the woman to email her some photos of Emily. Her head was churning with possibilities. She had already thought of a few things she wanted to try out.

"Aren't you taking on too much?" Star asked over dinner. "When was the last time you talked to Nick?"

Jenny stared at her pan seared fish moodily. Her aunt was right. She hadn't caught up with her son in a while. She just assumed he was busy with his classes.

"Nicky doesn't want me pestering him all the time."

"Checking up on your kid once in ten days isn't pestering," Star preached.

Jenny took Star's words to heart. She took her cell phone with her when she went for her walk.

"Is that the ocean I hear?" her son asked. "Where are you, Mom?"

"Trying to walk off the half dozen donuts I ate today," Jenny groaned. "How are you, Nicky. When are you coming home?"

"Are you throwing a Halloween party?" he asked cheekily. "We have our very own skeleton to prop up in the garden."

"Don't joke about it," Jenny sighed. "But seriously, that's not keeping you away, I hope. You're not scared of coming home, sweetie?"

"Of course not, Mom! How old do you think I am? I'm up to my ears in midterms and assignments. I'm coming as soon as I turn in my last exam. Promise."

"Can you be here for the read-a-thon? We need people."

Nick knew all about the read-a-thon. He promised he would try to be there. Jenny suspected he had already discussed the event with Adam's twins.

Jenny spotted her biggest admirer in the distance. Tank leaped in the air and almost toppled Jenny, giving her his usual wet welcome.

"I missed you," Jenny said, hugging him.

"Tank doesn't know how lucky he is," Adam said drily.

He leaned on his cane and looked hungrily at Jenny. They sat in the sand, watching the waves lap against the shore.

"I feel so fortunate," Jenny sighed happily. "I never dreamed I would have a house on the beach."

"Where did you go on vacation?" Adam asked her.

Jenny didn't like to talk much about her past life.

"Here and there," she said evasively.

She had spent many summers in Europe, waiting for her husband to join her. The expensive vacations any woman would covet hadn't brought much joy to Jenny.

"The twins are up to something," Adam said. "Did Nick say anything to you?"

"My guess is they are coming here for the read-a-thon."

"Must be something more than that."

Heather ran up the café steps the next morning, tugging at Tootsie's leash. She tied her black poodle to a post. Tootsie burrowed in the sand and settled down for a nap.

"You're grinning like a Cheshire cat," Jenny commented as she gave Heather the once over.

"Oh Jenny, I'm on cloud nine."

Heather whirled around on her toes and beamed at Jenny.

"Hot date?" Star asked.

Betty Sue clacked her needles and muttered under her breath.

"Hotter than you can imagine," Heather breathed.

"Wait till you hear about it."

"Watch it, girl," Betty Sue railed. "We don't want any indecent talk here."

"Oh Grandma, you'll want to hear this."

"Where did you go this time?" Molly asked with a laugh. "Delaware?"

"Hush, Molly." Heather's high watt smile hadn't dimmed at all. "I'm dating a doctor."

Betty Sue sat up when she heard that.

"Where did you find a doctor to go out with you? On that Internet?"

"Actually, yes. I did find him online. But guess where he's from?"

Five faces looked at her expectantly.

"Pelican Cove!"

Molly burst out laughing.

"You went out with old Dr. Smith? Did you take him to a game of Bingo?"

"Not Dr. Smith!" Heather pouted. "Dr. Costa. Dr. Gianni Costa. He's the new hottie in town."

"You mean that young doctor who's moved here from Mexico?" Petunia asked.

"That's the one," Heather nodded. "And he's not from Mexico. He just lived in a border town before he came here."

"Isn't he old, dear?" Petunia spoke.

"He looks young. Age is just a number, anyway."

"So you are going to date someone old enough to be your father?" Molly asked.

"He's not that old," Heather said with a huff. "You guys are just jealous. Wait till you see him."

There was a shout from the beach. A tall, dark haired man waved at Heather. Molly and Jenny craned their necks to get a good look at him.

"He's coming here," Heather said, turning a deep red.

She waved back at the man and cupped her hands over her mouth.

"Over here, Gianni!"

Betty Sue was shaking her head and staring at her granddaughter in disbelief.

The man ambled over the boardwalk and walked up

the café steps. Tootsie let out a growl but he didn't stop to pat her. His coal black hair was the same color as his eyes. The diamond stud in his ear sparkled in the morning sun. He wore a light pink shirt over chinos. The top three buttons of the shirt were undone, exposing a broad chest matted with curly black hair. A thick gold chain sporting a big medallion hung around his neck.

Jenny decided Gianni looked unlike any doctor she had ever met.

"Hello ladies," the man said, flashing his pearly whites. "Heather has told me so much about you."

"How long have you known my girl?" Betty Sue asked suspiciously.

"Ah, you're Heather's grandma," Gianni said, picking up her hand. "You're the queen of this beautiful island I now call home."

He kissed Betty Sue's wrist lightly and placed a hand on his chest.

"Now I know where Heather gets her looks."

The Magnolias stared at Dr. Gianni Costa as if he was from another planet. He gestured expansively with his hands as he spoke. He had a compliment for every one of them. Then he kissed Heather's cheek and promised to see her later.

"So? What do you think?" Heather crowed as soon as he was out of sight. "Isn't he a keeper?"

Chapter 19

Jenny chatted with Captain Charlie. The breakfast rush kept her busy. She noticed Ricky Davis sitting out on the deck when she went out to get some fresh air.

"Good Morning," she greeted him. "Out of muffins again?"

Ricky pointed to his plate. Jenny saw two of the lemon blueberry muffins she had baked that morning.

"I wanted to talk to you," Ricky said, looking over his shoulder. "Is now a good time?"

Jenny went in and made sure Petunia could handle the counter. She came out with a fresh cup of coffee and sat down before Ricky.

"What's on your mind?"

Jenny could sense Ricky's nervousness across the table. A trickle of sweat ran down his forehead and he wiped it off with the back of his hand.

"You said something about the past month or two of Keith's life."

Jenny encouraged him to go on.

"Something happened. My mother doesn't know about this."

"I can keep your secret," Jenny said, "as long as it's harmless."

"Keith had been sober for the past three years. I already told you that. He had been off the radar for some time. Somehow he got wind of the fact that we sold Seaview. Either that threw him off or it was something else. He must have started using again."

"How did you find this out?" Jenny asked.

"He was arrested for drug possession," Ricky sighed. "He called me. I came and bailed him out."

"Where did this happen?"

"Up the coast in Maryland," Ricky explained. "I had to get back home immediately. Keith promised me he would come home to Texas."

"But he didn't?"

"Looks like he stayed on in the area. I guess he eventually turned up in Pelican Cove."

"Are you saying Keith might have taken the drugs himself?"

"No! He would never do that." Ricky looked at Jenny

in despair. "I don't think he did that."

Jenny tried to be gentle.

"None of us want to believe he took his own life. But this changes things. Keith did have access to drugs, apparently. I think you should talk to the police about this."

Ricky looked sad and guilty.

"I should have stuck around. Or insisted he went home with me."

"You couldn't have known." Jenny knew anything she said at this point was just a platitude.

"Mother doesn't know any of this. She will be heartbroken if she finds out."

"I'm glad you came to me with this information," Jenny told Ricky. "You did the right thing."

Jenny couldn't stop thinking about Keith as she went about her work. She wasn't ready to accept he had taken his own life. Other than Ann or Ricky, there was no one she could suspect. Jenny decided she needed to find out more about Keith's time in Pelican Cove.

Mrs. Turner emailed her a bunch of Emily's photos as promised. Jenny spoke to Adam about it that night.

"Do you think she's out there, Adam?"

Adam had a suggestion for a change.

"Why don't you use one of those software programs that tell you how a person would look in a certain number of years? Then show that photo around."

"We can print an ad in local newspapers," Jenny said eagerly. "And I can post it online too. Ask people to share it."

Jenny tried to put herself in Emily's shoes. What if she had run away from home? What would she do? Her face broke into a smile as she thought of something. Chances were slim but Jenny didn't have much else to hold on to.

Heather had invited everyone to drinks at the Rusty Anchor. They hadn't gone out as a group in a long time. Jenny reluctantly agreed to go.

"You need a change of scene," Heather convinced her. "Let your hair down for a change."

Chris and Molly sat hand in hand, talking softly to each other. Jenny felt like a third wheel and wished Adam was coming. Heather arrived with her latest friend, the colorful Dr. Costa. Jenny noticed the fourth button of his shirt was undone, his nod to the evening hour.

Dr. Costa took over the conversation and soon

everyone was in splits. Jenny had to admit she hadn't laughed that much in a while. Eddie Cotton came over with another round of their drinks.

"I need to go," Molly said. "I have an early day tomorrow."

"Are you taking time off for the read-a-thon?" Jenny asked curiously.

"I'm trying to make up for a day's work," Molly told her. "I'm taking two days off."

"I hear Ricky Davis is back in town," Eddie Cotton, the proprietor of the Rusty Anchor said as he wiped a glass.

"You know him?" Jenny asked sharply.

"Our families used to be tight," Eddie nodded. "My grandpa and old man Davis grew up together. He was bummed when the old man perished in the storm."

"So you knew Ricky back when he was a baby."

"Ricky's been in and out of Pelican Cove a lot," Eddie nodded.

Jenny climbed up on a bar stool and devoted her attention to Eddie.

"What are you doing there, Miss Jenny?" Gianni Costa

hollered. "We need you here."

Heather was practically sitting in the good doctor's lap. Chris Williams was staring at her with his mouth open. Jenny realized Heather was getting brazen by the day. They needed an intervention. She made a mental note to plan a girls' night soon.

Jenny turned her back on the rambunctious couple and faced Eddie.

"Wait a minute ... are you talking about the time Lily ran away?"

"Ricky came here at that time," Eddie nodded. "Stuck around with Lily's boy. That was back in the 90s. I'm not talking about that."

Jenny's heart skipped a beat as she urged Eddie to go on.

"Ricky was here last week. Him and Keith, just like old times. I poured them a pint myself."

"This was just before Keith died, right?"

Eddie frowned. "Yeah. A day or two before that, I guess. Must have been the last time they saw each other."

"Are you sure about this?"

"Of course I'm sure. I just serve the drinks, Jenny. I don't touch the stuff."

"That scumbag," Jenny muttered under her breath. "Any idea what they were talking about?"

"I don't know," Eddie shrugged. "They got into a row after some time. I heard your house mentioned."

"Seaview?"

Eddie's nod was answer enough.

Jenny marched into Jason's office next morning.

"Did you know about this?" she demanded, glaring at him with her hands on her hips.

"Calm down, Jenny, take a load off."

"That scoundrel Ricky, he's been lying to me all along."

Jason pulled a cold bottle of water out of his small refrigerator and put it before Jenny. Jenny ignored it.

"Eddie Cotton told me all about it. I should have gone to the Rusty Anchor sooner."

"Why don't you begin at the beginning?" Jason's calm voice finally forced Jenny to simmer down.

"How many times have we asked Ann and Ricky about

their whereabouts?"

"At the beginning, Jenny!"

"Ricky was here last week. He was spotted in town a day or two before Keith died."

"What was he doing here?"

"Arguing with Keith over Seaview."

"You don't know that for sure." Jason stared at her in disbelief.

"I don't," Jenny agreed. "But those two were fighting alright and talking about Seaview."

"What was there to fight about?"

"Money!" Jenny exclaimed. "It's obvious they sold the house without his knowledge. Wanna bet they were planning to run with the loot?"

"We bought Seaview at a very reasonable price, Jenny," Jason reminded her. "Nothing exorbitant, considering how big the house and the land is."

"And your point is?"

"Ann and Ricky are very well off. So was Keith or his father. They didn't really need the money from the sale."

"I guess they would have sold the house long ago if they needed the money," Jenny thought out loud.

"Ricky told you about his separation. I think he was thinking of coming to live here. Ann was dead set against it. She thinks the house is jinxed."

"So she sold it?"

"You made the offer, remember? It came at the right time for Ann Davis. She wanted to get rid of the property before Ricky was tempted."

"And what about Keith?"

"Keith never cared for the place either. Don't know what made him come here now."

"That's another mystery we will never solve," Jenny sighed.

"What do you want to do now?" Jason asked her.

"I can confront Ricky about this, but how is it going to help?"

Jason shook his head.

"Don't do that. Let him think he got away with it."

"Got away with what?"

"We don't know that yet ... don't jump to

conclusions."

"Shouldn't we tell the police about this though?"

"Tell Adam. Let him decide how he wants to handle it."

Jenny picked up the bottle of water and drank from it deeply.

"You're looking exhausted, Jenny," Jason said with concern. "Is something bothering you?"

Jenny had a glimpse of the old Jason.

"I could use a vacation. I'm busy baking and prepping for the read-a-thon. Nothing's moving on the Keith front. Emily Turner's mother has asked me to find her. We still don't know anything about Mrs. Bones. Nicky hasn't been home in weeks. Heather's turning into a hussy."

"Calm down and take a breath," Jason laughed. "You're carrying too much weight on your shoulders."

"I can't get anything done, Jason," Jenny wailed. "I'm worried about the concession stand we are setting up. What if no one turns up? All that food will be wasted. Or what if we run out of food?"

"It's all going to be fine," Jason said, taking her hand and stroking it. "You're not alone, Jenny. The

Magnolias are with you. So am I. And Adam, for what he's worth."

Jenny finally smiled.

"Forget all this stressful stuff. What is this I hear about Heather?"

"Have you met Dr. Costa yet?" Jenny asked with relish. "Gianni Costa?"

The two friends spent some time catching up on what was happening in town.

"How's Kandy?" Jenny asked. "Haven't seen her in a while."

"She's busy working on a big case. She'll be in town for the read-a-thon though. She's looking forward to it."

Jenny made her autumn chicken salad and made a couple of sandwiches with double scoops of salad. She added two slices of chocolate raspberry cake for dessert and put it all in a basket.

"No need to hurry back," Petunia told her. "Your aunt is coming over for lunch."

Nora, the clerk at the police station greeted Jenny like an old friend. Jenny knocked on Adam's office and went in, bracing herself for what he might say. Jenny could never predict Adam's mood. They were often controlled by how his leg was faring that day.

"You look just like the woman in my dreams," Adam said. "She brought me cake."

Jenny unpacked the basket, fighting to hide a blush.

"I need to tell you something," she began. "It's about Ricky Davis. He's been lying to us."

Adam held up a hand.

"It can wait. Let's eat first. You are wilting before my eyes."

Jenny snorted with mirth.

"Love is blind …"

She bit her tongue and turned red as a tomato. Adam stared at her, his eyes wide.

Jenny stammered to correct herself.

"I didn't mean … that is …"

"I know exactly what you mean," Adam said softly, giving her a goofy grin.

Chapter 20

Pelican Cove bore a festive look. A huge tent had been erected in the town square for the read-a-thon. Tables and chairs were set up, forming large reading areas. People had lent rugs and carpets. These formed cozy reading nooks, piled with abundant cushions. A smaller tent was set up as a food and drinks zone. Jenny had set up shop inside it.

There was a modest crowd present for the inauguration at 9 AM on the first day. Betty Sue Morse cut the shiny red ribbon pulled across the entrance to the tent and declared the festival open. The smattering of applause was drowned by the patter of feet as people rushed into the tent and took up positions. Everyone wanted to win the early bird prizes.

"We need more people," Barb Norton boomed. She stalked around like a drill sergeant, ordering the volunteers around. "Why don't you take control of the social media?" she ordered Heather. "As it is, you are glued to that phone all the time."

"I don't need my phone now," Heather giggled. "I have a boyfriend."

"Don't you mean sugar daddy?" Jenny teased. "Are you that desperate, honey?"

"Gianni's fun," Heather said lightly. "He's perfect for me."

"What about that social media?" Barb Norton reminded her.

"Okay, okay. I'll take some pictures and post them online."

"Take a picture of that hay wagon too," Barb ordered. "And tell them about the rides."

Heather scurried along, snapping pictures of people with their heads in their books. She started tapping on her phone and gave Barb a thumbs up sign.

"We have the first break in a couple of hours," Barb said, taking Jenny to task. "Have plenty of food ready and make sure the coffee's hot."

Jenny didn't need much prompting. She had her routine meticulously planned out.

Ann Davis walked up to the reading tent, leaning on Ricky's arm. They both sat down to read. A volunteer noted the time and wrote down their names.

Barb declared the early bird prizes just before lunch. A group of tourists turned up in the afternoon, intrigued by the novelty of the event.

"We already clocked five hundred hours," Barb

announced with a megaphone.

A cheer went up through the assembled group.

"How are the donations going?" Jenny asked her. "I still don't understand how all this works."

"People are donating a fixed amount for every hour. They choose the number of hours they want and the rate. It's easy to calculate their total donation."

"And they do this just because they want to help?"

Barb told Jenny she was being tiresome.

The Boardwalk Café did brisk business and the concession stand was a hit. Tourists flocked to the café after they tasted the food at the concession stand. Jenny put on a second batch of chicken soup.

"What are you serving tomorrow?" a woman asked. "I hope you have a different menu for each day."

Jenny assured the woman and started listing the weekend's menu on a chalk board.

"We are spending the weekend on the shore and we want to taste the local delicacies."

The woman asked for recommendations for dinner and Jenny told her about Ethan's Crab Shack. The read-a-thon was turning out to be quite a crowd puller.

It was going to be a lucrative weekend for the whole town of Pelican Cove.

"Call for you." Petunia's voice broke into Jenny's reverie.

It was Adam, wanting to know if she was free for dinner.

"I'm going to be here till eight. I don't think I will have the energy to do anything after that."

"And here I was hoping for a romantic date."

Jenny didn't want to disappoint Adam. She gave in easily and asked him to Seaview for dinner. Star came in just before she hung up.

"Jimmy and I are going out," she announced. "You have the house to yourself."

"You don't have to leave on my account."

"Actually, we need some privacy," her aunt said with a wink.

Jenny had no response for that.

Barb Norton came into the café with Dale at her heels.

"Have you thanked the man who made all this possible?" she beamed. "Dale says the read-a-thon is a success."

"You have already surpassed what we accomplished for the whole event. And the first day isn't over yet."

"You were a big help, Dale." Barb patted him on the back and looked at Jenny expectantly.

Jenny and Star hastened to compliment the man.

The read-a-thon wound down at 8 PM. Jenny directed people to the Rusty Anchor and Ethan's place for a quick bite. She thought about what she could make for dinner as she walked home. She decided on a quick shrimp pasta.

Adam lit candles in the great room at Seaview while Jenny showered upstairs. She had set the table but he wanted to do something special for her. He went out and built a quick bouquet of flowers using the roses and gardenias she loved so much.

He went inside and poured the local wine he had brought along. Jenny had liked this particular wine when they went out before. He was ready for her when she came down the wide sweeping staircase.

Jenny took a deep breath and hesitated on the final step. She clutched the banister nervously as Adam handed her the flowers with a flourish.

"Thank you," she said, taking a quick sniff.

Dinner proceeded a bit awkwardly. They hadn't spoken to each other since her giant faux pas at the police station. She wasn't sure how Adam was going to handle it.

"Are we going to talk about what happened?" Adam asked, almost reading her mind.

"I wasn't thinking," Jenny said quickly. "You don't have to feel obligated."

"I don't," he assured her, taking hold of her hand.

"You have come to mean a lot to me, Jenny," he said hoarsely. "Maybe we should wait until we start assigning labels to this."

Jenny mentally sighed with relief.

"Whatever you are comfortable with," she said, bobbing her head.

"You know I'm not good with words," Adam said. "But I can feel what we have is special. I want to keep it that way."

"There's no rush, Adam." Jenny took a big sip of wine to bolster her courage.

"You are not going anywhere, are you?" Adam smiled. "Neither am I."

"That's right," Jenny agreed. "So we'll take it slow."

That seemed to clear the air. Adam asked for a second helping of pasta and they ate voraciously, doing full justice to the fine meal.

"Do you want to sit out on the patio?" Adam asked. "It's a fine night."

They stepped out into the garden, Jenny stopping to get a wrap for herself. The contractors had finished installing all the features in the garden. They sat on a swing, watching the gurgling stone fountain, the gold and russet fallen leaves and the ocean waves crashing against the shore.

"I hear the read-a-thon is a success?" Adam spoke, twirling a strand of Jenny's hair in his fingers.

"How could it not be? It's Barb Norton's pet project."

"What about your projects? Have you done anything to find that missing girl?"

Jenny had put some things in motion. But for the first time, she didn't expect anything to materialize out of her efforts.

"I am pretty sure that girl does not exist."

"Did you tell that to her mother?"

"You think I should have? I think the woman is prepared for any outcome. She just needs closure. Maybe you can give it to her when you get an update on Mrs. Bones."

"Why are you so sure about this?"

"Keith had to be involved." Jenny shook her head. "Ann and Ricky knew about that girl. Keith was obsessed with her, madly in love."

"Why would he kill her then?"

"We're back to the same point."

"Motive is important, Jenny. If Keith was so much in love with that girl, why did he kill her?"

"I don't have an answer for that. But he came here, didn't he? He came here because of the skeleton. I am sure about it. Something spooked him."

"He might have thought like you. He thought the skeleton was his girlfriend. He came here to find out."

"Who else would have wanted her dead?"

"What about her family?" Adam asked.

"Her family knew nothing about Keith, or so they say. In their eyes, she was a good girl who sang in the choir and was going to an Ivy League college."

"Learning about her real life would have been a shock," Adam pointed out. "What if they killed her in a fit of anger?"

"And did what? Brought her here? Why? To put the blame on Keith?"

"As long as we are considering wild theories," Adam said drily, "think about this. What if they followed her here? They found her with Keith. There was some kind of fight and the girl died."

"What about Keith? Think he would have kept quiet about it all these years?"

"They could have forced him to," Adam said thoughtfully. "Maybe that's why he came here. Once they found her, there was no need for him to keep the secret."

"Keith was in deep shock after Emily went missing. Ann said he started doing drugs after that. He spent his life roaming around the country, possibly looking for his Emily."

"Poor guy," Adam sighed.

He settled into the swing and put an arm around Jenny's shoulders.

"You think love lasts a lifetime?"

Jenny thought of the twenty years she had spent worshipping her ex-husband. Her whole life had revolved around him.

"I used to," she murmured. "Now I'm not so sure."

"What about the Davises?" Adam asked after a while. "Any idea why they are sticking around in town?"

"I know, right? What are they doing here for so long? Ricky says they are taking a vacation. But why now, after all these years?"

"How is it you haven't suspected Ricky yet?" Adam asked with a smile.

"I don't trust him." Jenny decided she had to tell Adam about Ricky's alibi. "He was here in town just before Keith died."

"What are you saying?" Adam asked sharply. "Are you sure?"

"Eddie Cotton told me. Ricky was at the Rusty Anchor with Keith."

"When were you planning on telling me?"

"I was going to," Jenny apologized. "But I know you believe the suicide theory."

"I still do, but this might be worth looking into."

"I feel we don't know enough about Emily Turner."

"I thought there was plenty of information about her."

"It's not enough." Jenny believed Emily would provide the missing piece of the puzzle. "Look, we know Keith loved Emily. He carried her picture in a locket for twenty five years. But did Emily love him?"

"What are you getting at now?" Adam asked.

"What if Keith's attentions were unwanted. Emily felt trapped and ran away."

"She could just have filed a complaint for harassment," Adam said, dismissing the idea. "Or talked to her parents."

"She was sixteen, Adam. She must have been scared out of her wits."

"So what? She ran away from home? That doesn't make sense."

"Keith must have known where she lived. Wouldn't he have gone there looking for her?"

"If he did, her parents would have known about him."

Jenny thought about Mrs. Turner and the photos on her mantel. Emily had been her perfect little angel. Had the woman managed to shut out anything unpleasant about her daughter?

"How do you feel about a little road trip?" Jenny asked.

"You think a man in uniform might make them talk?" Adam asked.

Jenny smiled and hoped Adam would remember his promise the next day.

Chapter 21

Jenny and Petunia started baking at 5 AM. They had a few trays of muffins and donuts ready for the concession stand before the usual breakfast rush started.

Jason came in with Kandy. She wasn't wearing one of her power suits for a change.

"We thought we would get breakfast here. We are going to read for the rest of the day."

"How about those famous crab omelets?" Kandy asked with childlike enthusiasm. "Jason can't stop raving about them."

"Can I talk to you?" Jenny asked Jason after serving them. "It's about Keith."

"Sure." Jason sprinkled some Old Bay seasoning on his fluffy omelet and cut a piece. "What's on your mind?"

"Someone mentioned Keith had a trust fund. Who gets all that money now that he's gone?"

"It depends," Kandy spoke up. "Did he have a will?"

Jenny wasn't too pleased with the interruption. She tried to hide her displeasure.

"We don't know anything about it."

"His father's still alive, right? If Keith didn't make a will, his father gets it all as next of kin."

"But he's incapacitated," Jenny reminded Jason.

"Well, in that case, the money will eventually go to whoever the old man's heir is. He might have appointed a trustee to handle his estate."

"Someone like Ricky Davis?"

"Could be anyone," Jason shrugged.

"So Ricky could be coming into a lot of money now that Keith is dead."

"You think Ricky Davis killed Keith for his money?" Jason asked skeptically. "Sounds farfetched to me."

Jenny agreed. She was beginning to think Keith's death was going to remain a mystery. Her gut feeling told her his killer was still out there. She wasn't ready to accept he had taken his own life.

"What are you planning to read?" Jenny asked Kandy. "Not law books?"

Kandy assured her she had a list of bestsellers she needed to catch up on. Jason and Kandy walked out of the café, arm in arm. Jenny felt a tiny twinge of jealousy but she ignored it.

"Are you ready?" Petunia asked.

Petunia had hired a few people to carry the food over to the concession stand. There was a big rush for breakfast before the first reading session started. Jenny put in a few hours, reading her old favorite - Treasure Island.

Adam sauntered over just as the lunch rush was winding down.

"Someone mentioned a road trip."

"Can we grab a bite first?" Jenny's feet ached and her stomach grumbled.

"Do you want to eat at Ethan's?" Adam asked.

"Tempting, but this will be quicker. Let me make a sandwich for us."

They sat on the deck, eating the chicken salad sandwiches Jenny had quickly put together. She packed two cupcakes for the road and poured fresh coffee into travel mugs.

Adam looked at Jenny as they drove out of town.

"Have you thought about what you want to ask them?"

"I'm going to wing it. I want to make her open up. Let's hope your presence does that."

"Are you saying I am intimidating?" Adam teased. "You talk like I'm an ogre or something."

"If they are hiding something, the sight of your uniform might rattle them."

"I checked with the forensics lab. They are running tests on your Mrs. Bones. We should know something soon."

Jenny hadn't called ahead. It was all part of her plan to catch Mrs. Turner at a disadvantage. She hoped the woman would be home.

Mrs. Turner stared at them with puffy eyes when she opened the door. She shivered when she spied Adam.

"Have you found her?" she gasped. "Have you found my Emily?"

Jenny hastened to explain.

"Calm down, Mrs. Turner. We are just here to ask you some questions."

The woman stumbled as she led them inside. Jenny held her by the shoulders and led her to a chair. The woman looked like she had been crying. An empty box of Kleenex lay toppled on the coffee table. A bunch of crumpled tissues littered the carpet and the couch.

"Have we come at a bad time?" Jenny asked nervously. "I am sorry we didn't call ahead."

All her bravado had deserted Jenny. She could almost feel the pain radiating from the older woman. Jenny wasn't sure how she could console her.

"Today's her birthday," the woman broke out in a sob. "My baby's birthday. She would have been 42." She looked up at Jenny. "About your age, I think."

The woman was off by a few years but Jenny didn't correct her.

"Do you celebrate her birthday every year?" Jenny asked.

She was really curious.

"We used to, for a few years." Mrs. Turner had pulled herself together. She pulled a fresh box of tissues from under a table and dabbed at her eyes. "Now I just bake a cake. My husband finds it silly, you know."

"That sounds wonderful," Jenny said, trying to cheer her up. "Did she like cake?"

"She loved desserts," Mrs. Turner said, brightening up. "She wanted red velvet cake for her birthday every year." A fresh stream of tears rolled down the woman's eyes. "Red was her favorite color."

Adam coughed and cleared his throat. Jenny imagined he was feeling uncomfortable with this open display of grief. Jenny debated going back home without asking any of her questions. She didn't want to prey on a helpless woman. Then she told herself she had to be strong if she wanted to find out the truth.

"Can I get you something?" Jenny asked Mrs. Turner. "How about a cup of tea?"

The woman led Jenny inside. They came back a few minutes later, carrying a tray loaded with a teapot and some cups. Jenny poured the tea and handed it around. Mrs. Turner looked better after a few sips.

"I hope you will pardon me," she began. "I'm sorry you had to see all this drama."

Jenny assured her she understood.

"What brings you here?" Mrs. Turner asked. "Have you found something?"

Her eyes filled with anticipation and she leaned forward eagerly.

Jenny shook her head sadly.

"It's too soon, Mrs. Turner. I had some more questions for you. I can come back later if you don't feel up to answering them now."

"I already told you everything about Emily."

Jenny nodded at Adam. He pulled out the chain from his pocket and handed it over.

"Have you seen this before?" Jenny asked.

Mrs. Turner took the chain from Jenny and looked at it.

"Looks like some cheap trinket. What does this have to do with my Emily?"

"Why don't you open that locket?" Jenny asked.

The woman found the clasp and the locket sprang open. Her eyes popped out of their sockets as she spotted the photo inside.

"Emily!" she whispered hoarsely.

Her head sprang up and her gaze moved sharply between Adam and Jenny.

"Where did you get this?"

"Do you confirm this is your daughter, Mrs. Turner?" Adam asked.

"Yes, Yes," the woman almost screamed. "This is my daughter Emily."

"We recently had a suspicious death in Pelican Cove," Adam explained. "This chain was found in the dead man's room. We are guessing he must have known your daughter."

"Dead man?" the woman mumbled.

She looked so bewildered Jenny had to believe her surprise was real.

"His name was Keith Bennet," she said, watching Mrs. Turner keenly. "He used to live in Pelican Cove."

"Keith ..." the woman muttered. "How could it be?"

"Did you know him?" Jenny asked sharply. "Did you know Keith Bennet, Mrs. Turner?"

Mrs. Turner gave a slight nod.

"We heard that he was in love with your daughter. In fact, he loved her so much that his life went awry when your daughter disappeared. He started taking drugs. He drifted around, possibly searching for her. Do you know any of this?"

"You don't have to tell us anything," Adam warned. "But we need to know the whole truth if you want us to find your daughter."

Mrs. Turner looked like she was going to lose her composure again. But she pulled herself together.

"We knew she met someone from out of town," she admitted.

"Why didn't you tell me this before?" Jenny demanded.

"My daughter was perfect. Do you blame me if I want to preserve that memory?"

"Was she really perfect," Adam drawled, "or did you just want her to be?"

"How did a sixteen year old go meet a boy in a town ten miles away?" Jenny pressed.

"She hitched rides," Mrs. Turner said under her breath. "Emily met this boy somewhere. I don't know how. But he got into her head. He was older than her, almost 19. That makes a big difference at that age."

"You didn't approve?"

"We thought he was a bad influence."

"You said she hitched rides," Adam stepped in. "Do you realize how dangerous that can be? Did you tell that to the police when your daughter went missing?"

"We didn't want to tarnish her reputation," the woman said. "Look, Emily was a good little girl all her life. She followed the rules. Then she turned sixteen and everything changed for the worse. She started staying out beyond curfew. She didn't tell us anything."

"So age was the only thing you had against Keith?" Jenny asked.

"He was madly in love with her. You could say he was obsessed. We felt Emily was too young to seriously commit to anyone."

"What did Keith want? Wasn't he in college at that time?"

"He wanted to marry her," the woman burst out. "How ridiculous was that?"

Jenny wondered if Keith had always been a bit weird. Had Lily's disappearance pushed him off the edge?

"He had suffered some personal setbacks that year," Jenny told the woman.

"We knew that. We felt sorry for the boy. But what could we do?"

"Did he ever threaten Emily?"

"Not to my knowledge," the woman said. "Do you think he hurt my baby?"

"We can only speculate."

"Did Emily bring him here to meet you?" Jenny asked.

"No, she never told us about him."

"Then how did you find out?" Adam asked.

He had been following the conversation quietly.

"We tried to keep tabs on her," Mrs. Turner said. "We had to, once we learned she was going out of town without telling us."

"Did you have her followed?" Jenny asked, trying to hide her disgust.

The woman nodded.

"She didn't like it but what were we supposed to do? We wanted her to be safe."

"But the inevitable happened anyway," Jenny murmured. "So did you ever meet Keith?"

"He came here," Mrs. Turner explained. "Three days after she went missing, he came looking for her."

Jenny and Adam sat up.

"What did he want?" Jenny asked urgently.

"She was supposed to meet him one night but she never turned up. He thought we had held her back."

"Was that the first time you saw him?"

"Yes. We were surprised he came here. He thought we had sent Emily away. He begged us to let him meet her."

"Did you believe him?" Jenny asked eagerly. "Or did you think he was putting on an act?"

"My husband and son were convinced he had hidden her somewhere. But I thought he was telling the truth."

"Did you tell the police about him?"

The woman shook her head. Jenny wondered about how much the Turners had managed to keep from the police. Then she thought of Mrs. Bones and felt her heart race. If that was Emily, they would learn her fate soon enough. But would they ever find her killer?

She looked up at the mantle crowded with photos of a beloved daughter. Her gaze fell on an old black and white photo. A young boy and girl stood arm in arm, smiling into the camera. The face struck a chord with Jenny.

"Who's that?" she asked Mrs. Turner, walking over to the mantle to point at the photo frame.

"That's my son," the woman said proudly. "He is two years older than Emily. They were like two peas in a pod."

Chapter 22

Jenny could barely sit still on the ride home. She wanted to know what Adam was thinking.

"Do you agree he must be involved?"

"Hold your horses, Jenny," Adam cautioned. "Don't jump to conclusions without any proof."

"Are we going to get that proof?"

Adam looked grim as he took his foot off the gas pedal to accommodate a slow moving car.

"Why don't you leave this to the police now? You have done enough."

"I will gladly do that. Will you promise to look into this right away?"

"I need to sit down and revisit the whole thing."

Jenny rolled her eyes and turned her head to stare out of the window. Adam could try her patience. But at least he wasn't ruling out her theory like he usually did.

"You have to agree he had a motive?" she pressed Adam. "All this time, we hardly had any suspects. It's all clear now."

"So you think he took revenge," Adam sighed. "You think he would do something so dramatic after all these years?"

"He loved his sister. He has been grieving over her for twenty five years. It's like a wound that festers."

"If you're right about this, he could be dangerous." Adam was grim as he glanced at Jenny. "I want you to promise me you will stay out of this."

"Okay, Okay. I won't go looking for him."

"Try not to be alone," Adam continued. "Stay with Molly or Heather at all times."

"Are you going to lock me in a room now?"

Adam shook his head in frustration and muttered to himself.

"I just want you to be safe, Jenny. I don't want anything to happen to you."

"I'll take care," Jenny promised reluctantly.

Although she wasn't sure what she would do if she came face to face with the killer.

The read-a-thon was in full swing when they got back to Pelican Cove. There was a line at the concession stand and Petunia looked done in. Jenny hurried to relieve her.

Molly walked up, looking for something to eat. "I put in six hours since this morning," she bragged. "I need a break."

"Remember what I said," Adam reminded Jenny as he walked off to the station.

"You're hiding something," Molly squealed, peering at Jenny through her thick Coke-bottle glasses. "Spill it."

Jenny changed the topic by asking Molly what she had read.

"I already finished Pride and Prejudice, Emma and Mansfield Park. I am reading Persuasion now."

"So you're on track to win that Austen prize," Jenny said.

Molly was excited.

"Chris and I are looking forward to a romantic dinner in the city."

Barb Norton walked up with Dale in tow.

"Hey Jenny!" she exclaimed. "Anything left for us?"

She picked up a muffin and started peeling off the paper.

"You have done an excellent job with the food. Half the people said they came here to taste your desserts."

"Thanks for setting all this up, Barb," Jenny said sincerely.

The older women Jenny called friends were not too keen on Barb Norton. But Jenny could give credit where it was due. The success of the event proved Barb deserved any praise they could heap upon her.

Barb beamed up at Dale and patted his arm.

"This is my secret weapon. Dale has helped me so much, Jenny. You know he is the mastermind behind this whole concept. We would never have come up with such an event without Dale."

Dale seemed to puff up with pleasure. He kissed Barb on the cheek and grinned widely.

"The people of Pelican Cove really came through."

The look he directed at Jenny was full of admiration. Jenny smiled back, trying to gauge the real expression behind his baby blue eyes. Was she looking into the eyes of a killer?

There was a shout for help from the tent and Dale Turner walked away to handle it.

Ricky Davis came out of the tent, holding Ann's hand.

They looked like they had been having a good time. Ann's face lit up when she spotted Jenny.

"How about some hot coffee, young lady?" she asked. "And I wouldn't mind one of those cakes. Reading is hungry business."

"Are you enjoying yourself?"

"Very much," Ann said happily. "Whoever put this thing together did a very good job."

Barb Norton sprang forward and introduced herself to Ann.

"I need to bring out a fresh batch of cupcakes," Jenny said to Ricky. "Walk with me?"

If Ricky had harmed Keith, confronting him was going to be dangerous. Jenny convinced herself her promise to Adam was limited to staying away from Dale.

"You lied to me, didn't you?" Jenny asked calmly, as she pulled out a fresh tray of cupcakes out of the big refrigerator.

"Huh, what?" Ricky stammered.

His face was mottled with red spots and sweat beaded his brow.

"You were spotted arguing with Keith just one day

before he died. Are you going to deny that?"

Ricky leaned against a chair and sat down with a thud.

"Look, it's not what you think."

Jenny folded her arms and raised an eyebrow.

"I'm listening."

"We were in the area, visiting a cousin near Washington DC. Keith called me. I thought he was in trouble again."

"What did he want?"

"He insisted I come to Pelican Cove to talk to him."

Jenny pulled out a chair and sat down herself.

"What was so urgent?"

"That's how Keith was," Ricky said bitterly. "He was missing from the scene most of the time, but when he did turn up, he needed constant attention. You can say he demanded it."

"Why did you humor him?"

"He was the closest thing I had to a brother," Ricky said.

Jenny sensed regret in his voice.

"I loved him, despite what he turned out to be."

Jenny gave Ricky a few moments to settle down.

"What did he want this time, Ricky?"

Ricky smiled mirthlessly.

"This concerns you in a way. He wanted us to buy back Seaview."

Jenny thought of what the place meant to her.

"I would never have done that."

"He told me he was working on you. He was very confident he would convince you to sell."

"He told me the house was jinxed and it would bring me a lot of grief."

"That was his way of trying to scare you into submission."

"So my hunch was right. You sold the house to me without Keith's permission."

"It wasn't like that. He never cared about the place. He never expressed any affection for it."

Jenny didn't think Ricky was lying this time.

"So that's what the argument was about? Seaview?"

"Keith told me about the skeleton they found in your garden," Ricky said reluctantly. "He was convinced it was Emily."

"So that's why he came here to Pelican Cove!" Jenny exclaimed. "What happened afterwards?"

"I tried to convince him to go back with me. He said he had unfinished business. I told him Emily was gone and he needed to move on. That didn't sit too well with him."

Ricky told her they parted ways after that. Ricky drove back to his cousin's home, hoping Keith would come to his senses and join them there. Two days later, Keith was dead.

Jenny was too exhausted to go out for her walk on the beach that night. The final day of the read-a-thon brought a hefty crowd of tourists to town. Jenny scurried around, working in the kitchen, dishing out food and volunteering some reading time in between.

A small stage had been set up to announce all the prizes. Betty Sue sat on the stage, next to Ada Newbury. Dale sat next to them, wearing a suit and looking important.

Barb gave away all the small prizes and announced the total numbers. A cheer went up through the crowd. Jenny spotted Adam moving through the crowd, along with two policemen. They handcuffed Dale and took him along with them.

Jenny was hopping with excitement, wondering what was going on. Adam came to talk to her. Heather, Molly and Chris stood next to Jenny, wondering what was going on.

"We did some good old fashioned police work," Adam told them. "Dale was found stalking Keith a couple of times. He was very bold. Molly's neighbor, old Mrs. Daft, spotted him going up the stairs to Keith's room.

"Do you think he will confess?" Jenny asked with concern.

She need not have worried. Faced with all the evidence against him, Dale started talking.

Adam held Jenny's hand as they walked on the beach that night. They both wore sweaters to ward off the chill.

"Why did he do it?"

"Justice for his sister," Adam said. "Just like you thought."

"So he always suspected Keith?"

"He used to follow them years ago," Adam explained. "Just to keep an eye on his sister."

"That sounds creepy."

"Emily was really young, I guess. If the twins had fixated on some older boy when they were sixteen, I might have done the same."

Jenny knew Adam was right. Parents always wanted to protect their children from wrongdoing.

"Dale read about the skeleton they dug up at your house. He had his suspicions. He came to town offering to help with the read-a-thon. He saw Keith at your café. All the memories came flooding back."

"Did he confront him?" Jenny asked. "Did he give him a chance to defend himself?"

"Dale wanted Keith to admit he killed Emily. Keith maintained he was innocent. Dale worked himself into a frenzy. He went to Keith's room. Keith was lying asleep with a syringe by his bedside. The temptation was too much for Dale."

"Does he regret it?"

"He thinks he got justice for Emily."

Jenny told Adam about the message she had received that day. She had a hunch about what was coming.

A middle aged woman walked into the Boardwalk Café two days later. Her brown hair was faded and streaked with gray. The crow's feet around her eyes made her look a lot older than she was. She sat down at a table near the window.

Jenny walked up to her with a tray of coffee and muffins.

"How was your drive?" she asked.

"Nostalgic." The woman smiled drily.

"I'm glad you decided to come here, Emily."

Emily Turner looked at Jenny with eyes as blue as her brother's.

"I think I've done enough damage. If only I had come to my senses a few weeks ago, or a few months ago."

"Are you ready to talk about it?" Jenny asked gently.

"There's not much to say." Emily's voice was heavy with sadness. "I was a headstrong sixteen year old with stars in my eyes. I was attracted by the bright lights. I wanted to be a rock star."

"Your mother knew none of this?"

"My parents thought I was their pretty little girl. They didn't want me to grow up. I was tired of living up to their expectations."

"Parents only want the best for their kids," Jenny said softly.

Emily shrugged.

"What did I know? Then there was Keith. He followed me around like a puppy. He wanted to marry me. I wasn't going to marry him at sixteen! And what, throw my life away cooking and cleaning for him?"

"So you planned it all?"

"I used to hitch rides to come to Pelican Cove," Emily told Jenny. "I met a group of musicians. They traveled around the country, playing gigs in small towns. They heard me sing and offered to take me on."

"You fell for it."

"I was so hemmed in, you know. I felt trapped between my parents and Keith. I just wanted to fly and spread my wings."

"Why didn't you ever call? Let them know you were okay? Your mom still cries for you."

"I came to my senses just weeks after I left. My life went downhill. I got pregnant and lost the baby. Then I got into drugs. I couldn't face my parents after all that."

"So the time was never right." Jenny felt sorry for the

woman sitting before her.

"What's the use of coming back now?" Emily asked in an anguished voice. "I can't save Dale."

"Your mother's still waiting for you," Jenny told her. "She just wants to know you are okay."

"Were you confident I would come back?"

Jenny thought of the ads she had strategically placed in the local newspapers.

"Actually, I was convinced you were buried in my backyard."

Epilogue

The town of Pelican Cove was ablaze with the splendor of fall. The trees were painted in an array of bright colors, the reds, golds and yellows forming a sharp contrast to the blue-green ocean and the cerulean blue skies.

A party was in progress in Jenny's garden. The roses bloomed at Seaview and their scent mingled with the salty breeze coming off the ocean. The new water fountain gurgled merrily, spraying anyone who ventured close with a fine mist.

Jenny's son Nick had come home for the party. He was arguing about something with Adam's twins. Heather pouted in a corner, sulking because Jenny hadn't invited Gianni Costa to the party.

"He's a doctor!" she wailed. "Aren't you all happy I'm dating a doctor?"

"He's fifteen years older than you, girl," Betty Sue snapped. "Find someone closer to your age."

"He looks shady to me," Star added. "He wears more diamonds than I do."

The women laughed at that.

Jenny brought out a big platter of nachos. She had kept the menu simple. A taco bar had been set up with all the fixings. She was ready to put her feet up and drink fresh apple cider laced with spiced rum.

"So, you did it again, Jenny!" Jason Stone said, raising his glass at her.

Kandy was nowhere to be seen. Jenny had invited her for Jason's sake but she was busy working on a big case.

"Did Emily Turner go home?" Molly asked.

She sat next to Chris, her hand resting in his lap.

"She did," Jenny told them. "Her mother was overjoyed to see her. They are busy catching up."

"Ann was really generous, wasn't she?" Molly gushed.

Ann Davis had written a big fat check for the library. Coupled with the money raised from the read-a-thon and the amount promised by Ada Newbury, the library was now flush with funds.

"I don't have to worry about my job for at least three years," Molly said happily. "Dale Turner did something good after all."

"I don't know about that!" Jenny said uncertainly.

A phone rang somewhere. Adam walked over to a jacket lying on a chair and pulled his phone out. His face settled into a frown as he listened to the voice at the other end. He let out an expletive as he shut off the phone.

"That was my contractor," he told Jenny. "They are projecting a month to get all the work done."

Adam's roof had collapsed a couple of days ago. The twins hadn't been home and luckily, Adam himself hadn't been hurt. Jenny had invited him to stay at Seaview until he got his house back.

"I can't impose on you that long, Jenny," Adam protested.

"Why not?" Jenny asked with a smile. "There's plenty of room. And I like having you here."

"I live here too," Star said sternly. "So don't get any ideas."

She threw back her head and laughed. Jimmy Parsons laughed along with her.

"At least let me pay rent," Adam insisted.

"Now why didn't I think of that?" Jenny said mischievously. "I'll let you know how much you owe me, Adam Hopkins."

Adam looked scandalized.

"So we still don't know who Mrs. Bones is, do we?" Heather asked.

"Hush, girl. Think before you speak." Betty Sue glanced fearfully at the stone fountain.

"All we know is it was a woman around fifty years old. Right, Adam?" Star had no qualms talking about the skeleton.

"That's correct." Adam and Jenny were sitting on a wicker sofa, munching on nachos. "She's been buried for thirty years, give or take a few."

"I've been thinking about this," Jenny told the others. "It's just a hunch, but I think I'm right."

Nick and the twins stopped arguing and looked at her.

"Think about it." Jenny widened her eyes as she stared around the group of people. "A fiftyish woman who lived around here twenty five or thirty years ago? A woman who was never seen again?"

Betty Sue's face turned ashen and tiny beads of sweat appeared on her upper lip.

"You don't mean …?" she stared at Jenny helplessly.

Jenny nodded at Betty Sue, a sad expression in her

eyes.

"Lily!" Betty Sue spoke under her breath.

"Lily?" Heather exclaimed indelicately. "But she ran away with her lover."

"Did she?" Jenny voiced the question running through everyone's minds.

THE END

Thank you for reading this book. If you enjoyed this book, please consider leaving a brief review. Even a few words or a line or two will do.

As an indie author, I rely on reviews to spread the word about my book. Your assistance will be very helpful and greatly appreciated.

I would also really appreciate it if you tell your friends and family about the book. Word of mouth is an author's best friend, and it will be of immense help to me.

Many Thanks!

Author Leena Clover

http://leenaclover.com

Leenaclover@gmail.com

http://twitter.com/leenaclover

https://www.facebook.com/leenaclovercozymysterybooks

Other books by Leena Clover

Pelican Cove Cozy Mystery Series –

Strawberries and Strangers

Cupcakes and Celebrities

Berries and Birthdays

Waffles and Weekends

Muffins and Mobsters

Parfaits and Paramours

Meera Patel Cozy Mystery Series -

Gone with the Wings

A Pocket Full of Pie

For a Few Dumplings More

Back to the Fajitas

Christmas with the Franks

Acknowledgements

This book would not have been possible without the support of a number of people. I am thankful to my beta readers and advanced readers and all my loved ones who provide constant support and encouragement. A big thank you to my readers who take the time to write reviews or write to me with their comments – their feedback spurs me on to keep writing more books.

Join my Newsletter

Get access to exclusive bonus content, sneak peeks, giveaways and much more. Also get a chance to join my exclusive ARC group, the people who get first dibs on all my new books.

Sign up at the following link and join the fun.

Click here →
http://www.subscribepage.com/leenaclovernl

I love to hear from my readers, so please feel free to connect with me at any of the following places.

Website – http://leenaclover.com

Twitter – https://twitter.com/leenaclover

Facebook – http://facebook.com/leenaclovercozymysterybooks

Email – leenaclover@gmail.com

Printed in Great Britain
by Amazon